RAGS TO WITCHES

ALSO BY HP MALLORY:

PARANOMAL WOMEN'S FICTION:
Haven Hollow
Misty Hollow
Gwen's Ghosts
Midlife Spirits

PARANORMAL & FANTASY ROMANCE:
Witch, Warlock & Vampire
Ever Dark Academy
Lily Harper
Dulcie O'Neil
Gates of the Underworld

PARANORMAL REVERSE HAREM:
My Five Kings
Happily Never After

CONTEMPORARY ROMANCE:
Age Gap Romance

SCI-FI ROMANCE:
The Alaskan Detective

RAGS TO WITCHES

WITCH, WARLOCK & VAMPIRE
Book # 8

H.P. Mallory

SOMETHING WITCHY THIS WAY COMES

HP MALLORY

Copyright ©2018 by HP Mallory

All rights reserved. No part of this book may be used or reproduced in any manner whatsoever without written permission, except in the case of brief quotations embodied in critical articles or reviews. Please do not participate in or encourage the piracy of copyrighted materials in violation of the author's rights. Purchase only authorized editions.

Acknowledgments

My extreme gratitude goes to the following people:

My husband for your love and support
My mother for all your valuable input
Klaasje Helgren and Mercedes Berg who both won my "Become a character in my book" contest. I hope you enjoy your characters!
And to all my readers, thank you! I would not have come this far without your support!

ONE

A few hours after our marathon lovemaking session, I found myself alone. Sinjin had announced that the dawn was coming and he would have to leave me for the day. That was when it hit me. Sinjin and I would never witness the beauty of a sunrise together, never see the world bathed in that beautiful nascent pink. We would never spend the day at the beach, watching children play in the waves under an August sun. And speaking of children, Sinjin and I would never have any—vampires were unable to procreate. The more I thought about it, the more it bothered me.

Is everything in life a trade-off, then? I asked myself. Sinjin was basically the perfect guy in every way but one . . . he was a vampire. And even that was arguable, because there were aspects of his vampirism that could definitely be considered benefits. His incredible strength and speed, for one, and the fact that he could live forever . . .

Yeah, but you won't live forever.

I felt my breath catch, and I had to ask myself why this had only just occurred to me. I mean, the realization that I would grow old while Sinjin remained just as gorgeous and young as ever should have been one of my first thoughts after I'd discovered what he was.

I don't care, part of me declared. *Sinjin is everything I could ever want in a man. He's funny, kind, thoughtful, and extremely intelligent. He's protective, not afraid of commitment, financially well off, and incredibly attractive. And he's amazing in bed! I mean, what more could a woman want?*

Jolie, stop kidding yourself—you've always wanted a two-story house with a picket fence and two kids running through the yard.

But Sinjin was the only man I'd ever met whom I'd even consider as a possible partner for my "two-story with a picket fence" scenario. How cruel fate was, offering me someone so perfect when there was no chance of us having a real future together.

Besides, he's made it pretty clear that he isn't the falling-in-love type. I felt my heart sink.

Although it seemed as if Sinjin was falling for me just as, er, well, almost as quickly as I was for him, I still couldn't ignore the fact that he had *purposefully* announced he wasn't into admitting to any sort of love.

And, really, where did that leave me?

Don't give up on him, my optimistic side said. *Don't give up on him, because you are already in love with him.*

I took a deep breath at the very thought that I could be in love with Sinjin. Was I? Could I be? The more I considered it, though, the more I had to admit to myself that I absolutely was head over heels in love with him. I mean, really, how could I not be? He was basically like a knight in shining armor: someone who had ridden into my life and opened me up to a world I never knew existed, helped me see truths about myself I never would have otherwise known. There was a whole new world waiting for me, complete with creatures that had previously only existed in my dreams . . . or nightmares. And while that realization was frightening in itself, knowing that Sinjin would serve as my teacher and guardian somehow made it seem a little less daunting.

Sinjin Sinclair was my sworn protector, teacher, friend, confidant, ally, and lover. And I was in love with him—it was as obvious as the fact that he was a vampire.

Then why should it matter that you won't be able to have his children? I asked myself.

Hmm, I guess maybe it doesn't matter . . .

And furthermore, what do you care if you never watch a sunrise or sunset with him? Sunlight isn't all it's cracked up to be anyway, you know. It's responsible for freckles, sunburns, skin cancer . . .

Okay, okay, I get it. I paused at the realization now dawning within me. *I guess I'm okay with loving Sinjin and seeing where it will go.*

But what about my getting older while he stays young?

Hmm, that was a problem that I couldn't discount quite so easily. But I also didn't need to solve it today.

I climbed out of Sinjin's bed and took a deep breath, looking down through the window as the sun's beams glittered on the pool's surface, looking like thousands of diamonds. I turned back to the king-sized bed; half the linens were twisted up on the floor, and the fitted sheet hung off one side of the mattress. I smiled to myself and set about making the bed, almost regretting the fact that I was destroying evidence that I'd had the best sex of my life last night. I couldn't help the flush that stained my cheeks. According to Sinjin, he'd never forget our first night together; I knew I wouldn't either. It was chiseled into my memory, and I already looked forward to replaying it endlessly.

I scanned the room for my clothing and I found the garments strewn around as haphazardly as if a hurricane had blown through the room. Still in a sex fog, I dressed slowly, and once I was decent, I opened the door,

My lovely little poppet,
Your breakfast awaits you in the kitchen.
Last evening was magical and I am most excited to repeat it this eve.
I will dream of you.
~ Sinjin

I couldn't help the smile that curled across my lips. I folded the note into a small triangle and put it in my pocket, knowing that I'd refer to it countless times today—to reread it and to admire the neat curlicues and flourishes of Sinjin's calligraphic handwriting.

I took the stairs two at a time and entered the kitchen, where a bouquet of red roses was sitting in a vase of water on the black granite countertop. Beside that was a plate full of croissants, biscuits, muffins, and Danishes; beside those was a bowl containing a mound of melon slices, grapes, strawberries, and bananas.

"Wow, Sinjin," I whispered with a smile as I plopped a few grapes into my mouth, helping myself to a croissant. I took a seat on one of his bar stools and leaned over to smell the roses. This whole thing was just so unbelievable—such a perfect fairy tale. Wasn't this exactly what every woman dreamed of—a man, er, a vampire, as amazing as Sinjin in the looks department who was also just as caring?

And suddenly I was angry with myself—angry that I'd ever doubted the future of a relationship with Sinjin in the first place. He was just so incredibly sweet and good. And what was more, he made me happy. In fact, I couldn't remember the last time I'd been this completely content, this thrilled with my life.

After finishing the croissant, a handful of strawberries, and a few melon wedges, I couldn't eat any more. I got off the stool and searched through the kitchen drawers, looking for some Saran Wrap, but found them completely bare. Reluctantly, I put the uncovered bowl of fruit in his fridge, which was just as empty as the rest of his kitchen, and, grabbing the bouquet, started for the door. I made up my mind to stop off at Bed Bath & Beyond on the way to my shop and get Sinjin all the accoutrements of a well-stocked kitchen. Granted, he probably wouldn't ever use any of them, but I would.

Beeping my Jetta unlocked, I closed Sinjin's door behind me before having second thoughts and locking it. I mean, it was daytime, after all, and Sinjin couldn't protect himself. As soon as that thought dawned on me, I felt bogged down with worry. Sinjin was basically as helpless as a turtle on its back during the day. Hmm, we would have to have a discussion regarding his safety this evening . . .

I jogged across the street, got in my car, and started it as I glanced at the clock.

"Shit," I said, remembering that my first client of the day was due in twenty minutes. My trip to Bed Bath & Beyond would have to wait until my lunch break.

I peeled out into the street and gunned it, happy to find that I didn't hit any red lights on the way. When I pulled up to my store, I noticed Christa's red Camaro in front and breathed a sigh of relief that she'd managed to open the store on time. Her punctuality was usually fifty-fifty. I parked behind her, grabbed the bouquet, and sprinted to the front door.

"Ahem," she said as she glanced up at me, an irritated frown marring her pretty and otherwise perfectly made-up face. I handed her my purse, which she accepted and put underneath the counter, where we both kept our bags. "Did someone forget it was a school day?"

I smiled guiltily. "Um, yeah, sort of lost track of time."

She narrowed her eyes on me and cocked a brow as her gaze dropped to my neck. "Looks like Mr. Vampire got a little carried away."

My hand immediately rose to my neck, where I felt the two telltale punctures. I hurried to the bathroom and looked in the mirror, turning my head to the side to see how bad the damage was. The two bite marks were red and raised, looking swollen and irritated. "It's bad," I said once I noticed Christa behind me.

She handed me the pink scarf I insisted she keep in the drawer underneath the cash register. Why? Because Christa had come into the store more than once with hickeys all over her neck. Luckily for me, the hickey wrap was now going to come in very handy.

"Did it hurt?" she asked.

"No . . . well, maybe a little but I barely noticed because we were . . . doing other things."

She sighed and shook her head, crossing her arms against her chest. "So he finally got some vag?"

I glanced over my shoulder at her and frowned. "Oh my God, Chris, do you have to be so . . . so gross?"

She sighed. "Okay, so he finally got to lick your cupcake?"

I laughed. I couldn't help it. And then, remembering the moment when Sinjin devoured my so-called cupcake, I smiled, feeling a blush steal across my cheeks. "Yeah, you could say that."

"And you didn't even call to tell me?" she demanded, following me into the front of the store. I glanced at the clock on the wall and noticed we had five minutes until my client was due.

"Well, I didn't really have time to call you, Chris." I shot her a look over my shoulder. "I mean, I am late this morning, in case you didn't notice."

She muttered something unintelligible, but I couldn't say my mind was on her. Instead, I couldn't help but focus on the beautiful woman who had just walked through my front door.

With her arms crossed against her chest, she didn't look happy. Well, happy or not, she was unarguably stunning. She looked like one of those femme fatales in the James Bond movies—perfect hourglass figure, large breasts, tiny waist, and generous hips. Her oval face finished in a square jaw and extremely high cheekbones, which emphasized her incredibly shapely, full lips. Her hair had a reddish tinge but was overall dark, and she had to have the most beautiful skin I'd ever seen. She was dressed in fitted black slacks and a low-cut, ivory satin blouse with heels that were so high, she appeared to be over six feet tall.

But despite her incredible beauty, there was something hard about her, something bitchy.

"Which one of you is Jolie Wilkins?" she asked, glancing between us. She had an American accent, which surprised me; her looks gave her a certain foreign vibe.

"Um, that's me," I answered and stepped forward.

She arched a brow at me, taking me in from head to toe and frowned, seemingly unimpressed. "Sinjin sent me."

"You know Sinjin?" I asked, feeling my heart plummet to the floor. Almost immediately, jealousy began to well up within me.

How does she know Sinjin? And furthermore, why is Sinjin carrying on with such an incredibly beautiful woman?

They must have been an item in the past. Who knows, maybe they're an item now?

Don't think that or you'll just drive yourself crazy. Besides, it isn't fair to Sinjin to just make assumptions.

Remember what happens when you assume. You make an ass of u *and* me.

I shook my head, forcing the voices to shut the hell up.

"Yes, I know Sinjin," the mystery woman said hurriedly, like it was a given since she was here and he'd apparently sent her.

"Who are you?" I asked, not liking the fact that she knew who I was and yet I had no clue who she was or why she was here. "And why did Sinjin send you?"

She glanced at me and then at Christa, as if she wasn't sure if she should say certain things in front of my friend.

"Whatever you have to say to me, you can say in front of her," I managed.

The woman narrowed her eyes. "I'm Bella Sawyer, and I'm here to perform a protection spell on you."

"You're a witch?" Christa piped up, sounding like a five-year-old, excitement brewing in her tone.

Bella faced her but said nothing, merely scowled. It was pretty apparent she was a witch, and just then, I registered her electric blue aura, which I hadn't even noticed. No, I'd been too busy sizing her up and feeling dejected and jealous all at the same time.

Apparently dismissing Christa as unimportant, she faced me again. "Sinjin told me about your little visit from the warlock, which is why I'm here."

"Rand," I said. She nodded, taking a few steps closer to me as she eyed the surroundings of my store and frowned with distaste.

"Yes. Apparently Sinjin doesn't want a repeat of Rand's last visit. That's why he called me."

"When you say a protection spell . . ." I started.

She huffed, apparently annoyed that we weren't getting down to business. But before anyone put any sort of spell on me, I had to understand just what that meant.

"Think of it as a magical restraining order. The warlock won't be able to get within twenty feet of you."

I felt myself sigh in relief, grateful that Sinjin seemed to think of everything. Just as quickly as the relief overwhelmed me, another feeling reared its unwanted head, which was hard to describe. It was maybe something of a cross between regret and sadness. I trampled the feeling down, though, because it was ludicrous.

Rand wanted to control me. Sinjin had said so himself. I glanced at Bella as it suddenly occurred to me that maybe I shouldn't be so trusting of her either. I mean, how did I know Sinjin had sent her and not Rand? Maybe this was some sort of setup, and she was really going to drug me with her witchcraft. Who knew where I'd end up? "How do I know you are who you say you are or that you were really sent by Sinjin?"

Bella frowned and glanced at her watch, obviously wanting to get the message across that she had places to go and people to bespell. Well, join the club. I still had a client who was probably going to walk in any second.

"Check your cell phone," she ordered. "You should have a message."

Surprised, I glanced at Christa. She reached for my purse underneath the counter, handing it to me. I fi shed through it until I found my cell phone. I clicked the voice-mail button and listened.

"Good morning, my love," Sinjin's voice rang out. "A witch under my employ, Isabella Sawyer, will be visiting you today. I apologize for not giving you adequate notice but I am worried by the warlock's visits. Isabella is a very capable witch and will ensure your protection. I apologize that I could not introduce you both in person. I do hope you understand." He paused for a second or two. "Last evening was magical, little poppet."

He hung up and I turned the phone off, facing Bella. "I didn't know he'd called."

She frowned again. "He contacted me early this morning before the sun came up. Apparently you were sleeping." Then she eyed me up and down again, her expression one of repugnance, as if she were beholding Jabba the Hutt. She was, no doubt, shocked that girl-next-door me was now Sinjin's newest flavor. At that moment I knew Bella Sawyer and I would never be friends. And it was also at that moment that I realized that she realized Sinjin and I were sleeping together. I couldn't seem to find it in myself to be embarrassed.

She clapped her hands together as if we were now moving to step two.

"Do you believe her?" Christa asked me, reminding me that she was still in the room. She was eyeing Bella with daggers.

I smiled at Christa, appreciating the fact that my best friend was so protective. Then I glanced at Bella and nodded as I approached her. "We can go in the reading room."

"Um, you do have another client coming in soon," Christa announced.

I gulped and nodded, thinking this might be an issue. "Can you just have him or her wait for a few minutes?"

"Her," Christa corrected.

"Maybe offer her some coffee and make small talk," I finished.

Chris nodded and glaring once more at Bella, returned her attention to the *Vogue* magazine that was spread out on the counter.

I started for the hallway, Bella just behind me.

"I'll be out here if you need me," Christa called.

"Thanks, Chris," I answered as I faced the reading room. When I opened the door, the darkness seemed to accost me; it took a second or two for my eyes to adjust to the red light bulb that fought against the otherwise pitch blackness. Approaching the reading table, I pulled out the chair for Bella as I took a seat on the opposite side.

She motioned for my hands. "I need to touch you in order for the spell to work."

I nodded, giving her my hands. I felt a slight pinch of electricity flow through me, which automatically reminded me of the first time I'd touched Rand— how his electricity had jolted through me and how overcome I'd been by my feelings toward him.

Do you think this could be a mistake? I heard my inner voice.

No, Rand wants nothing more than to control me, and who knows how desperate he'll get. Who knows what he's capable of.

But what if what he said was true? What if you really should trust him? What if those feelings you get around him are valid?

They aren't. Now stop talking, stupid voice!

"So Rand won't be able to ever get near me again?" I asked, suddenly impatient to get this show on the road.

Bella closed her eyes and nodded. "That's the plan."

"How foolproof is this?" I continued, worry lacing my voice. Hey, it wasn't like I'd ever been on the receiving end of a spell before . . .

She opened her eyes as she dug her nails into my hands. "I am an extremely powerful witch," she barked, clearly offended. "It's foolproof."

I swallowed hard. "I didn't mean to insult you."

"Close your eyes," she said, obviously still affronted. "And focus on receiving my power."

"How do I do that?"

She shook her head and grumbled something unintelligible. "Just clear your mind, and for God's sake, stop talking."

I frowned but closed my eyes and did my best not to think of anything, which was damn hard to do. My brain instantly switched into overdrive with thoughts of everything from what I was going to eat for lunch to what relationship this woman had with Sinjin. Finally I was able to focus on the blackness of my eyelids.

"It's done," Bella announced and dropped my hands, standing up.

I glanced up at her in surprise. "That's it?"

"Yes," she said impatiently.

"I didn't feel anything."

"You weren't supposed to."

Somehow I just couldn't fathom that there hadn't been any sign at all that I'd just been bewitched. I mean, she hadn't even chanted or done anything resembling hocus-pocus. "Are you sure you did it right?" I asked and then gulped at her expression of pure hostility. "There wasn't anything I was supposed to say or you were supposed to say or some potion I should have drunk?"

She started for the door. "I hope Sinjin knows what he's doing," she said and turned to face me, scowling as she exhaled her pent-up frustration. Then before I could respond, she walked out of the reading room. Moments later I could hear the sound of the front door closing behind her.

If I'd thought my dealings with Bella Sawyer were over, I was sorely mistaken. That evening marked meeting number two, and to say I was disappointed was an understatement.

After getting off work, going home and showering, feeding the cat and myself, I headed for Sinjin's. I wanted to throw my arms around him and forget the stresses of the day in his embrace. So you can imagine my frustration when he announced we were due at Bella's house momentarily. He escorted me to his Ferrari and, once we were en route, glanced over at me with that winning smile of his.

"Isabella is going to act as your teacher, love," Sinjin responded when I gave him a pouty face that said just how much I was looking forward to this.

"I thought you were my teacher," I replied.

He chuckled and shook his head. "There are only so many subjects I can teach you, my pet. Unfortunately witchcraft is not among them."

I just nodded but didn't say anything more. I glanced out the window, getting lost in the scenery as it blurred past, and wondered about my life. It was like I'd just woken up one day and everything was turned upside down. Well, more like inside out.

I felt Sinjin's hand on my thigh and glanced up at him. He smiled over at me as his attention moved from my face to my bust and down to my legs. "I dreamed of you today, poppet," he whispered.

"I didn't know vampires could dream," I said.

He just nodded. His eyes seemed to glow with the whiteness that meant that he was either angry or aroused. "I dreamed of being inside you, feeling you writhing beneath me."

I swallowed hard and damned Bella to hell for even existing. "Why do you have to talk like that when we aren't going to be alone anytime soon?" I demanded grumpily.

Sinjin chuckled. "All in due time, my pet, all in due time."

Before I could say another word, he pulled up in front of a plantation-style three-story home that looked like something out of a magazine. "Is this where Bella lives?" I asked, shocked.

"It is," Sinjin said as he turned the car off and opened and closed his door, materializing in seconds at my side. He opened the car door for me and helped me up, offering a chaste kiss on my lips as he closed the door behind me. "We will not tarry long."

I just frowned and accepted his arm as we approached the front door. He rang the bell and

Bella opened it instantly, pasting on a smile as soon as she saw him. Once she saw me, her smile dropped.

"What a pleasant surprise," she said in a way that made it pretty apparent there was nothing pleasant about the surprise at all. Well, about the me part of the surprise anyway.

"How did the spell go?" Sinjin asked and helped himself into her house. She stepped out of the way and looked pissed off.

"Do you doubt me?" she asked, obviously miffed.

He faced her and smiled. "Of course not." Then he turned to me and motioned for me to come in. "Poppet, stop lolling about."

I didn't say anything but nodded a small greeting to Bella and stepped into her vestibule, craning my neck as I took stock of my surroundings. She breathed out what sounded like irritation and started forward, Sinjin just beside her and me bringing up the rear. We walked into her living room and she took a seat on her sofa, crossing her legs seductively as she stared up at Sinjin. I couldn't catch his reaction since his back was to me, so instead I turned to take in the room's furnishings. The ceilings were incredibly high and with the white tile floors, white slip-covered furniture, and bright white walls, the whole place felt like a hospital—antiseptic and cold.

"Isabella, I want you to cast a spell in order to judge the Lurker threat," Sinjin said, all matter-of-fact and businesslike.

"And how do you propose I do that?" she demanded and stood up as if shocked by his request. "The spell requires more than one witch."

Sinjin smiled and glanced at Bella furtively. "One," he started and then turned to me. His smile broadened. "Two."

"She's hardly a witch," Bella said and harrumphed.

"She has more power than you could dream of," Sinjin responded, his tone icy.

Bella scowled at him and turned to face me. "Do you even know who and what the Lurkers are?"

I nodded, feeling like I was a student on the receiving end of a quiz. "Yes, they are humans with vampire powers and they want to kill all of you."

"Succinct," Bella said with distaste, as if I were a complete and total idiot. "Give me your hands."

I obeyed and awaited more direction.

"Because you cannot visualize a Lurker, given that you have never seen one, all I need from you is your energy," Bella started. "I want you to close your eyes and funnel your power, your energy into me. I will do the rest." Then she turned to face Sinjin. "We will see if she has enough power within her."

Sinjin said nothing but glanced at me with a wink.

"How do I funnel my energy into you?" I asked, facing Bella.

"Each witch has her own way of channeling her power. I find it easiest to imagine pulling my energy from all parts of my body into my center. Then allowing it to spill out into whatever requires it, filling up a void." She narrowed her eyes at me. "Do whatever feels natural."

I nodded and closed my eyes, imagining any power that might actually be within me pulling into my center. It felt as if energy was suddenly springing up from my fingertips and feet, like tiny pricks all over my skin. It was akin to when your foot falls asleep and you have to shake out that feeling of pins and needles. I continued to imagine that energy moving to my middle; when I felt the busy hum of bees in my stomach, I then concentrated on sending the energy to Bella, bathing her in it.

I clenched my eyes shut as I felt the energy leave me—then I could suddenly see Bella before me, in my mind's eye. There was a cord of white light joining us, which I imagined was my power going into her. Even though my eyes were closed, I could see her as clearly as if they were open, which was odd to say the least. How that was even possible I wasn't sure, but I was also past the point of asking how and why. I mean, I *had* sort of accepted the fact that I was a witch. When my energy hit her, she jumped slightly and I could hear her intake of breath.

"I can see them, the Lurkers," she said in an awed sort of voice.

"How many?" Sinjin demanded.

"It is difficult to say but perhaps hundreds. They are building their numbers, concentrating only on replenishing their army."

"How are they building it?" Sinjin probed.

In my mind, I could see Bella shake her head.

"Dig deeper," Sinjin demanded. "Find out how they are adding to their battalions."

Bella nodded. "I need more power, more magic."

I figured that was my cue, so I focused even more resolutely, scraping up every last inch of whatever it was inside me that was fueling her abilities and sent it over to her. The white light around her glowed even more brightly.

"By way of magic," she said, sounding surprised. "It appears they blend magic with their own blood in some form of ritual."

"Are the victims taken by force?" Sinjin asked.

I felt myself swallow at the term *victims.*

"I can't tell," Bella answered. "I just have this feeling that there are many of them and they choose not to attack us because they are focused on growing their numbers first." She paused for a moment or two, then took a deep breath. "I believe there will be a battle, and it could be devastating for our kind."

Then she dropped my hands and I suddenly felt like I was going to pass out. I started to swoon and Sinjin immediately caught me. I blinked a few times, trying to clear the stars from my vision, and gazed at him in shock.

"Are you well, my pet?" he asked.

I nodded. "I think so. I just feel a little light-headed and weak."

Bella glanced at me and frowned. "It is to be expected. You just gave me all your power. It will take a few hours for it to return. Eat a large meal."

Frowning over the fact that I probably wouldn't be acquainted with a large meal in a long while, I tried to focus on the conversation and not the fact that I felt completely wiped out. "We will need to locate the prophetess," Sinjin said as he took a seat on her sofa, with me in his arms. He ran a hand through my hair as I relaxed against his chest, still feeling like I wanted to pass out.

"The prophetess?" Bella repeated, obviously surprised. "Impossible."

"Not impossible," Sinjin replied, smiling down at me as he did so.

"There are those who doubt her very existence," Bella continued.

Sinjin finally glanced up at her and there was impatience in his eyes. "I am not one of them."

TWO

The next day, I was back to feeling like myself—aka not about to pass out from sending all my life energy to the bitch, Bella. After we'd left Bella's, I'd questioned Sinjin about this so-called prophetess, but he hadn't admitted to much—just that she was some sort of super-witch and we needed her talents to help us combat the threat of the Lurkers. He'd also said that contacting her would be a feat and I wasn't up to it just yet: I'd need more lessons with Bella. So for the time being, I wasn't supposed to be concerned with prophetesses or Lurkers.

I took a deep breath as I stood behind the counter of my store while Christa prattled on about her last date and what a disaster it had been. I actually had been paying attention to her until I caught sight of a woman walking down the street. Ordinarily, I wouldn't have looked twice at a passerby, but this woman seemed out of place somehow, dressed in a white-and-yellow dress that skimmed the ground, the high collar and wrist-length sleeves looking like something out of *Little House on the Prairie.* Her incredibly long, flowing silvery hair seemed just as odd. She appeared to almost fl oat down the street even though she looked old and frail, like she was in her eighties. The closer she came, the more I realized her aura was beaming out of her in an exquisite bright blue. That had to mean one thing . . .

"Oh, fuck," I said under my breath.

"Are you listening?" Christa persisted as she took a seat on the stool behind the counter and stared at me with irritation on her face.

"No," I said rather absentmindedly. My mind, instead, was wholly focused on what to do about this woman. She was clearly a witch, or something similar. Her aura was the same color and intensity as Bella's and Rand's.

Rand.

Something warm flowered within me at the mere thought of his name. It was a feeling I couldn't categorize and didn't have time to, because the witch opened my front door.

"Hi, are you . . ." Christa glanced down at my appointment book, tapping her long, fake orange nails rhythmically. ". . . Mathilda?" she finished with an expectant stare.

The old woman nodded with a sweet smile at Christa before her gaze fell on me and she smiled even more broadly. I saw something like recognition passing through her intense green eyes. "Yes, I am," she said in a soft voice, the cadence of which sounded like the trilling of bells.

All at once the panic that was welling up inside me evaporated, leaving me with nothing but a feeling of complete trust. I felt sure this woman would never harm me. 'Course, by now I was also well aware that anything I might be feeling could be due to her witchcraft.

"Hi," I said, sounding a bit too harsh. I decided right then and there, however, that I didn't want this Mathilda woman to know that I knew what she was. Better to play it safe; and by *safe,* I meant dumb. "Are you ready for your reading?" I asked in a much friendlier, softer voice.

She nodded and offered me a charming smile. I forced a smile of my own, but all the while, anger was bubbling up inside me as I wondered what in the hell she wanted from me. All I knew was that I had to remember every second of what happened here today because I would report it back to Sinjin tonight.

I led her into the reading room and wondered if I should alert Christa to the possibility that this might turn out to be unpleasant. But then I thought better of it. It wasn't like Christa could do anything to help me; furthermore, I could be endangering her. No, I was just going to play it cool—find out what this woman wanted and send her on her way.

Once we entered the reading room, I shut the door behind us and lost sight of everything in the darkness for a few seconds until the glow of the red light overhead illuminated our surroundings again. I motioned to the small table in the center of the room and said, "Have a seat."

"Thank you," she responded, pulling out the chair. Her gnarled hand confirmed that she had to be pretty old. It was strange, though, because despite her advanced years, she appeared so statuesquely beautiful and serene. It was almost like her age made her more beautiful.

"Is there a particular person you were hoping to make contact with? Or did you want a card reading?" I asked as soon as we were both seated comfortably.

She smiled at me. "I was interested in you reading my cards."

Hmm . . . That surprised me but whatever. Besides, reading cards was way easier than trying to make contact with the dead. I grabbed the stack of tarot cards, unwrapped the red silk scarf from around them, and handed her the stack. "Please shuffle the cards, then choose seven of them, and hand them to me."

She nodded and separated the deck between her gnarled hands, carefully shuffling them four times. She cut the deck and then shuffled them another four times as if she had OCD or something. Then she removed two cards from the top, cut the deck again, and removed four cards from the middle, then the remaining card from the bottom, before handing them back to me.

When her skin touched mine, I felt a wave of electricity course through me, much like what I'd experienced with Rand. I abruptly pulled my hand back and realized I'd given myself away.

"I am not going to harm you, child," she said in a soft voice as she stared at me with her beautiful green eyes.

"Then what do you want?"

Her gaze didn't waver. "I am here to inform you that Rand is not your enemy."

"Oh my God!" I felt my face go white with fear as I realized she was one of Rand's emissaries. "So, what, he got too freaked out when I zapped his ass across the room and now he's sending his grandma to retaliate?" I wanted to throw her off the scent of the truth, which was that Bella's spell was protecting me. The less Mathilda knew, the better. Although, I had a mind to yell at Bella for not ensuring that all witches had to keep their distance from me. 'Course, then that would include her as well, I supposed. And maybe me too, for that matter. And how the hell would that work?

Never mind, Jolie! I yelled at myself. *All that matters is this woman! Find out what the hell she wants and get her out of here!*

"No, that is not why," she said simply.

"Let's stop beating around the bush then. What the hell do you both want from me?"

She took a deep breath like the answer was going to be long and complicated. "We want you to know the truth."

And then I remembered how anxious Sinjin had been when I told him Rand had come into my store and sent me that package—how he'd warned me that Rand was dangerous. I mean, Sinjin had taken major steps to ensure that Rand would have to keep his distance from me. So, as far as I was concerned, this woman might be equally dangerous. "You can leave now." I stood up, but she made no motion to follow suit.

"You need us," she said simply.

"I want nothing to do with you and I want nothing to do with that warlock. Do you understand?" I said, my voice deadly serious. "Now if you don't leave, I'm going to call the police."

She took a deep breath and rose from the chair, wobbling as she did so. I had the sudden urge to help her but another part of me wouldn't allow it. She was a witch or something magical—all of this was probably just a game, something meant to evoke my sympathy. Well, I wasn't going to fall for it.

"The vampire is not telling you the truth, child," she said in a soft voice.

I shook my head, although her comment made me apprehensive. Still, as soon as the worry reared its unwanted head, I shot it down. I just couldn't believe it—wouldn't believe it. Sinjin wouldn't lie to me. He was my protector, my teacher. He was the one person who had promised to guide me into this Underworld. He was the only one I could turn to, the only one I had.

And suddenly it seemed readily apparent that Rand had sent this old woman to shake my foundation regarding Sinjin. Her whole purpose was to weave lies and cause me to distrust him. Rand and this old woman wanted to woo me to their dark side. Well, I wasn't going to fall for any of their Jedi mind tricks. Yoda be damned. "Leave him out of this," I warned and started for the door. "And neither you nor the warlock is welcome in my store or anywhere near me ever again."

She reached out and touched my hand when she brushed past me. I felt my knees buckle, then I hit the ground hard. I had no time to even wonder at what the hell had just happened because her voice was suddenly in my head.

You must trust Rand and me. We are here to help you.

I tried to fight against her but she was too strong and the control she had over my mind and body was too powerful. I grabbed my head between my hands and closed my eyes, trying to force her out of my head. At the same time, I willed my legs to move, to stand up, but it was useless.

Everything you see around you is a farce, she continued. *It was never meant to be this way. The vampire broke the rules, Jolie.*

Images swarmed through my head like a hive of agitated bees. Images of Rand, of me in his arms, us kissing, dancing . . .

I shook my head, trying to clear the ridiculous visions because I knew they weren't real. How could they be? I'd never done any of these things! They were mere hallucinations—the work of a powerful witch—she was trying to implant memories into my subconscious that weren't real, memories that were fabricated by her.

"Stop!" I finally screamed, when I found my tongue again. But the sound came out as a weak whisper.

"Do not resist me," she said, softly placing her hand on my shoulder. As soon as she did, I felt myself surrender to her, suddenly weak. The images in my head slowed down, allowing me to focus on only one.

The vision appeared as any other, only the images were much more delineated and sharp. It took me a second to adjust, but once I did, I recognized my store. It was dark outside, the streetlamps already glowing yellow against the otherwise black night. I heard a sound to my right and glanced over to see myself as I busily readied the store for the next morning. So I was the omniscient eavesdropper in this vision? I didn't have time to further ponder it because the door opened. And that was when I saw him.

Rand.

I felt something catch in my throat and didn't want to even acknowledge it. But something like happiness filled me as soon as I saw him. Yet the feeling made no sense since Rand was my enemy.

I shook the feeling off and forced myself to concentrate on the vision. I watched myself greet him as if this were the first time we'd ever met. I wasn't afraid of him, which of course made no sense. This wasn't the way our meeting occurred at all. I mean, for one thing Christa had been there and it had been midday . . .

This is how it truly happened, Jolie, Mathilda's voice announced in my head. *You were destined to meet Rand first, not Sinjin.*

I wasn't able to argue with her. It was as if she were controlling my mind, showing me what she chose to. And there was nothing I could do to fight it. Instead, I watched myself unwittingly take Rand to the reading room. We sat down and I started to pull out the tarot cards, but he stopped me and asked me to read him instead. As soon as I touched his hands, that surge of energy coursed through me. I watched myself pull back in shock.

"I know all of this seems impossible," Mathilda said, her voice gentle. "But what you are seeing is real, and everything you know now is not as it was designed to be, Jolie."

I watched the vision fall apart before me and then I was back in my reading room, sitting on the cold floor. "That doesn't make any sense," I said, shaking my head.

Mathilda nodded. "Rand is the one who trained you to become a witch, child, who introduced you to this life," she continued. "He is not your enemy."

I shook my head. "So you're saying Sinjin is my enemy?"

She stepped back as I righted myself, leaning against the wall for fear I might topple over again. After a long moment of silence, I glanced over at her.

"Yes," she finished.

I shook my head, refusing to accept any of it. "I know what you're trying to do and it won't work. I will never, for one minute, believe any of this shit. Sinjin is not my enemy."

"He has brainwashed you to believe his lies," she argued.

"He hasn't brainwashed me into anything. He warned me about Rand. He told me how powerful and dangerous he is, so don't think I'm going to fall for your tricks."

She seemed surprised at that information and was quiet for a second or two. I, on the other hand, was another story—*how dare she come here and try to convince me to believe her lies! And, furthermore, how dare Rand send her here!* I needed to nip this right in the bud, if only to ensure I wouldn't receive any more visits from Sinjin's enemies.

"Sinjin and I are together and I trust him," I said. "So I suggest you and Rand don't ever come near me again or you'll have Sinjin to deal with."

She nodded as if she understood.

"Please tell Rand exactly what I've said to you," I finished.

"I will," she said softly. Before she left, she turned to face me again. She simply smiled and reached out, grabbing my hand. I flinched, and immediately tried to pull away, but her grip was too strong.

"See me not as I am and remember nothing," she said, and I struggled even harder. She released my hand and I suddenly felt myself falling backward.

It was like I blacked out or something. I shook my head and found myself on the floor of my reading room, looking around in bewilderment as if I'd just awoken from a cold faint.

"Are you well, dear?"

I glanced up at the face of the woman who had come into my store, looking for a reading. She offered her hand, as if such a frail creature could even hope to pull me to my feet.

"I . . . I think so," I said. "What . . . what happened?"

"You do not remember?"

I shook my head and felt slightly nauseous.

"You tripped, dear," the old woman said as she smiled down at me again. I stood up and leaned against the wall for support.

"Are you feeling okay now?" she asked again.

I nodded, not wanting to worry her. She held my hand and led me out of the reading room and back to the front room, where Christa looked up from buffing her nails.

"Your friend had a nasty fall, dear," the old woman said to Christa.

"Jules?" she asked and came around the counter. "Are you okay?"

I just nodded and allowed the old woman to lead me to the couch, where I sat down, still feeling woozy but more scared. It just wasn't like me to black out. God, what if I'd had a mini stroke or an aneurysm or something?

"What happened?" Christa asked as she took a seat beside me and held my hand. "Do we need to take you to the hospital?"

"No." I shook my head. "I'm fine, really. I think I just passed out."

I glanced up to thank the old woman but she was already gone. I looked to my left and right, but she was nowhere to be found.

"Where did she go?" I asked, baffled, a headache already starting between my temples.

Christa looked around herself and then shrugged, seemingly unconcerned. "She must have left, I guess." Then she faced me again. "Jules, are you sure you're okay?"

But I couldn't answer because I honestly didn't know.

The rest of the day went pretty much slower than a snail's pace and I couldn't wait to tidy up for the night so I could spend the evening with my vampire. Although, I had to admit that I needed to find a happy medium where sleep was concerned, because I was exhausted. Staying up all night and all day was too much for me to function properly.

Even though I felt like a sleep-deprived zombie, I couldn't hide the excitement coursing through me as I pulled up to Sinjin's house. I parked the Jetta in his driveway and glanced at my reflection in the rearview mirror, taking in my pink lips and shadowed eyes. Yes, I'd taken a few courses in the art of wearing makeup from Christa; we'd even paid a visit to the M•A•C counter in Macy's, where I spent way too much money. But there was now a part of me that wanted to look feminine and sexy. I shook my head, allowing the large blond waves to bounce around my face. Yes, I'd even gone so far as to curl my hair. Where the old Jolie Wilkins had retreated to was anyone's guess.

I unbuckled my seat belt, catching sight of my short, brown corduroy skirt, under which I'd worn tights with knee-high brown leather boots. And on the top? A skintight, camel stretch turtleneck that made my natural C-cup boobs look like D's. Or maybe that was just the Wonderbra.

I stepped out of the car and marveled over how much I'd changed. Two months ago, I wouldn't have been caught dead wearing this. Not that my outfit was too revealing or anything—it was just fashionable. And fashion and I had never been friendly. Well, I guess I could say we were now.

I opened the rear door and pulled out my overnight bag, a smile gliding across my lips at the thought that I had packed an overnight bag for Sinjin's. It just made things between us seem so . . . official—like we were definitely an item, boyfriend and girlfriend. Yep, I was going to spend the night with my boyfriend and we were going to make love all evening. I was so giddy, I felt like I might throw up all over my brand-new boots.

I slung the bag over my shoulder and, after beeping the car locked, I made my way to Sinjin's front door. Taking a deep breath, I glanced down at myself to make sure nothing was out of place. Then I ran my fingers through my hair once more, giving it an extra fluff before ringing the doorbell.

A few seconds later, the door opened to reveal my incredibly handsome vampire.

"Poppet," he said with that mischievous grin that characterized him so well. He was dressed all in black, as usual, his long-sleeved T-shirt doing nothing to hide the swells of his biceps or the mountains of his pecs. God, he was just so beautiful.

I stepped inside his house, dropped my overnight bag, threw my hands around his neck, and rose on my tiptoes so I could kiss him. He seemed taken aback at first, but then chuckled and draped his arms around my waist, sliding his tongue into my mouth. I groaned against him and met his tongue, thrust for thrust. I could feel him stirring beneath his pants and wondered if we might not even make it to the bedroom. But that thought was cut short when I heard the sound of someone behind me clearing her throat.

I squealed in shock as I pulled away from Sinjin and spun on my heel to face the intruder—Bella Sawyer! Son of a . . .

"Isabella," Sinjin said and smiled at her as if it didn't matter to him that she had just walked in on us in a passionate embrace. Based on her expression, she wanted to kill me right then and there. Hmmm . . . She was definitely jealous.

God, why can't I get away from this blasted woman? I asked myself. *And the bigger question— what is she doing in Sinjin's house?*

Actually, the bigger question is what's the history between them? That other voice reared up.

Do you think they used to date?

Oh my God, what if they're dating now? What if this is like that movie Dangerous Liaisons*?*

Well, Jolie Wilkins, you're definitely not killing yourself!

Despite the irritation snaking through me, mainly at Sinjin for having this awful woman in his house when he hadn't, at the very least, warned me, I remembered my manners and smiled. "Hi, Bella, it's nice to see you again." I mean, the American way was innocent until proven guilty, right?

Her feeble attempt at a smile came out as more of a sneer. "Hello again."

Not knowing what else to say or do, I faced Sinjin. "So, you never did tell me how, uh, how you two know each other?"

Sinjin closed the front door, drawing my attention to the fact that it had been open the entire time without me realizing it. As he walked back toward us, I noticed he was wearing black pajama pants and no socks or shoes. I gulped hard as images of the two of them in bed came crashing down on me. I pushed the images away, though, trying to force myself to be fair to Sinjin. Just because this hideous woman was in his house and he was in his jammies didn't mean he'd just screwed the hell out of her . . . Right? I mean, she was fully dressed, for crying out loud. Granted, her skintight, dark purple dress only went to her mid-thigh and was cut so low, I could see her navel, but still. I didn't even want to focus on her incredibly high, pointed stilettos; added to her already long legs, they made her look like she was descended from a gazelle.

"Isabella Sawyer and I go back many years, do we not, love?" he asked as he offered Bella his devil's grin. I felt myself swallow down a lump of resentment. I wasn't sure if the resentment was reserved for their long history or that he referred to her by the same name that he called me . . . *love*. Maybe it was both.

Bella sort of "hmmphed" at him and then nodded, her lips tight. "I suppose you could say that."

I tried to keep my temper under check, not wanting to paint this whole situation in a bad light, but little by little my patience was wearing thin. I mean, really . . . Why was Bella dressed so slutty and standing in Sinjin's house? With him in his pajamas! "I wasn't aware that Bella was visiting."

Sinjin took my hand and the cold of his skin surprised me for a moment or two, until his temperature warmed up to mine. "I invited Ms. Sawyer over this evening, poppet, to train you."

"Train me?" I asked, having momentarily forgotten that Sinjin had said Bella would have to train me in order for us to locate that supreme witch person.

"Yes, we have much work to accomplish if we are to locate the prophetess," he responded. Ah, that was it—the prophetess. "Isabella needs to teach you everything she knows—how to cast spells and do charms," he continued.

"Tonight?" I asked, aghast at the very thought. I'd been hoping for a quiet, romantic evening alone with my boyfriend and now Bella had been thrust into the mix? Really?

Sinjin pulled me closer to him, laughing into my neck as he did so. I watched Bella's hands fist at her sides and had never felt more uncomfortable in my life. Was Sinjin so unaware that this woman obviously had it bad for him? Or was he just playing with her heartstrings? I had to hope for the former because I couldn't imagine my caring vampire would sink so low as to toy with a woman's feelings. Either way, he definitely wasn't making it easy for her to like me.

"Shall we get started, then?" Sinjin asked with a large grin as he clapped his hands together and started down the hall. I noticed her raised-eyebrow expression as she apparently sized me up and found me lacking. She was quick to follow behind him as I took up the rear.

And just like that, my hopes for an awesome evening were crushed.

Sinjin led us into his living room, where I noticed he'd moved all of the furniture to the perimeter of the room. I was just waiting for him to bust out a pool filled with mud and tell us to go at it.

"Um, why did you clear everything out?" I asked dubiously, turning to face Sinjin.

"Because you, my dearest little poppet, are about to learn how to command your inner beast."

He might as well have been speaking Swahili for all the sense he made. "My inner what?"

He chuckled then, as if the whole thing were a big joke that I, stupid and uninformed Jolie Wilkins, didn't get. I exhaled a pent-up breath and felt my lips tighten as I watched Bella saunter toward us, hips swaying seductively. She stood very close to Sinjin—as in shoulders-touching close. I felt like I was playing the part of the third wheel, and doing a damn good job of it.

"Poppet, every witch has a wild beast within her that she can call upon when required," Sinjin explained.

"I still don't understand," I said, feeling my lower lip pout like a child about to have a temper tantrum.

"Witches can turn into animals," Bella finally said, sounding exasperated.

I looked at her like she'd just sprouted another head. Then I laughed, figuring the joke was totally and completely on me. People turning into animals . . . yeah, right. Yes, I had come to grips with the fact that witches and vampires weren't just the stuff of Halloween cartoons—but people taking the shape of animals? Then it occurred to me that werewolves probably also existed in this strange new world I called my life. "Um, so you're what, also a werewolf?"

Bella looked at Sinjin as if she was anything but amused, as if being called a werewolf was like being called a bitch or something. He just smiled at her, shaking his head. "Perhaps you should demonstrate?"

Bella's lips curled malevolently into what I suppose was the closest to a smile she could achieve. It was, however, dripping with something that was far from sweet. She then stepped away from Sinjin and walked to the center of the living room, swaying her hips like she thought she was Marilyn freaking Monroe.

"Remember your tail this time, love," Sinjin said, and chuckled to himself at what I imagined was an inside joke. I swallowed hard, not wanting to admit that there was nothing worse than an inside joke when you weren't on the inside.

I crossed my arms against my chest and watched Bella, hoping she would turn into some slathering, furry, flea-infested beast. I felt Sinjin come up behind me and wrap his arms around me, but I didn't change position. No, at this point, I was too pissed off. None of this made any sense. If I'd had any real balls, I would have just turned around and left when I discovered her here.

'Course, I was interested in what Bella planned to turn into, so I suppose my deciding to remain there was purely in the interests of curiosity. I watched her walk the perimeter of the room—and then she did something that defied logic, something that I don't even know how to begin to describe. She dropped to her hands and knees and, in a split second, became a lioness. There was no scrunching of bones, no snarling or sweating or anything that seemed to characterize the shape shifters you see in the movies. She was a woman one second and a lion the next. Her purple dress lay in scraps at her feet, obviously having not fared well in the transformation.

"Oh my God!" I screamed, not waiting around to decide if my eyes were deceiving me. Instead, I looked for the nearest exit. Sinjin laughed behind me and pulled me tighter into his chest.

"Shhh, my pet," he crooned into my ear. "She will not harm you."

I looked down at the lioness in front of me. She sliced the air with her paw, missing my leg by a few inches. Then she growled, so fiercely that I found myself climbing up Sinjin to escape. "She's going to kill me," I protested as I tried again to run away, but Sinjin held me in place, chuckling all the while.

"Come," he said to Bella, the lioness, and she purred immediately, allowing him to stroke her between the eyes. I wasn't sure if I should be jealous or not, considering they looked like Siegfried and Roy, but somehow jealousy did enter into the equation.

"I believe she is ready for instruction now," Sinjin finished.

With that, the lioness trotted back into the center of the room and lay down on the floor. Then, just as miraculously as before, she transformed, only this time it wasn't quite as spontaneous. Her long caramel-colored tail shortened into her backside while her claws recessed into human fingertips. Her rib cage decreased in size, now revealing only the outline of her ribs. Her two perfectly matched, very large breasts (D's by the look of them) were perky and completely real. She stood up and faced us both, naked.

In her nudity, she was absolutely magnificent. Great, just great.

"Um," I started, not really sure where to look. By the expression on Bella's face, she wasn't exactly shy when it came to standing completely naked in front of Sinjin or me. 'Course, I couldn't say any of this was for my benefit.

"Well done," Sinjin said, and I felt myself coloring. Whether or not he was getting pleasure from the sight of her flawless body was anyone's guess, but I wasn't a total moron so I had to imagine he was.

"Poppet, now it is your turn," he said as he pushed me away from him.

That was when I lost my temper. "If this is some plan you've concocted to have some freaking, weird threesome animal-style, I'm not into it at all." Then, feeling a bit more bravado after my outburst, I threw my hands on my hips and glared at Sinjin. "In fact, I've seen enough. So you two just party on down, but I'm leaving." Then I made for the nearest exit.

I heard the sound of Bella snickering, which was just as well. I wanted nothing more than to escape—to lick my wounds in the comfort and privacy of my own little home, to bemoan the destruction of my relationship with Sinjin. I hurried down the hallway, grabbing my overnight bag from the corner, and was about to throw open the door when Sinjin materialized instantly in front of me. I walked headlong into his chest and sucked in a surprised gasp of air.

"Get out of my way," I said.

"Is my little poppet jealous?" he asked with a big smile.

I felt something in me breaking. So he was going to tease me about this, was he? "I don't want to talk to you anymore, Sinjin. I want to go home."

"Please," he started.

"No, this whole thing was shitty on your part." I tried to sidestep him but he grabbed both my arms and wouldn't let go.

"I apologize for offending you, love."

"Stop calling me that."

"I do not understand," he said.

So I decided to make him understand. I dropped my bag and stepped back, away from his hold. Surprisingly, he released me. "Let me help you then. First off, it's not okay that you surprise me with that awful woman in your house and especially"—I glanced down the hallway to see if we were alone, which we were—"especially when she's dressed like that and you're dressed like that!" I motioned to his pajama bottoms. "Second, you should have warned me ahead of time that Bella was going to be here because that was just incredibly disrespectful, not to mention suspicious. And third, it is totally not okay that she's parading around completely naked and, even worse, that you seem to be enjoying it!"

He smiled slightly, as if my little freak-out session amused him, but when I bent down to pick up my overnight bag, his smile disappeared. "Please accept my humblest apology, love," he started. "And for the record, I cared no more for her demonstration than you did."

I looked at him in disbelief. I'd have to be the biggest idiot in the world to be buying any of this bullshit. "Please. I'm smarter than I look." Then it dawned on me that he'd just called me "love" again. "And I don't want to hear you call me 'love' ever again, when it obviously doesn't mean anything!" I railed against him, feeling my voice choking with tears.

"Calm down, poppet," he whispered and pulled me into his chest. "I see now where I went wrong and I cannot express how sorry I am. Please believe me that Isabella means nothing to me. We are merely old friends."

"You really expect me to believe that?" I asked incredulously.

He nodded. "Yes, because it is the truth. You are the only woman for me, Jolie." The way he said it screamed of honesty. There was no smirk on his face, no arrogance in his eyes, nothing. "You have always been the only woman for me."

I faced him and sighed, my guilt reminding me that acting the part of the jealous girlfriend was probably unwarranted.

No way, Jolie, jealousy was most definitely warranted here, and you did the right thing, I corrected myself. But somehow my anger had managed to simmer down. Maybe it was due to his confession that I was his only one. "Sometimes you say things that I just don't know how to argue with."

"How can I make this situation more comfortable for you?" he asked with sincerity. I knew he was being straight with me; his eyes showed no deceit or subterfuge. "We need Isabella, poppet, to instruct you; but I understand your reservations."

"Well, for starters, you can tell her to put some clothes on," I said angrily, but my slight smile softened the bite of my bark.

He chuckled and threw his arm around my shoulders, grabbing my bag and looping it over his opposite shoulder. Then we sauntered into the living room again where Bella was sitting on the couch and dressed in a tight black mini skirt and a plunging red halter top. She had magicked the outfit, if I had to guess—I hadn't seen her with a change of clothing.

"Is your little outburst over?" she asked with a sneer.

"Isabella, we shall have no more of your foul mood," Sinjin said with authority. Bella turned a surprised expression his way but said nothing.

"What does turning into a beast have to do with finding the prophetess anyway?" I asked grumpily.

Sinjin glanced down at me and smiled reassuringly. "They are not necessarily related, love, but you will need to hone your magic, cultivate it, in order to attempt to locate the prophetess. This is just one avenue to allow your magic to grow, to encourage it and strengthen it so you will be prepared when the time comes."

"I have places to be so let's get this over with," Bella announced as she glared at me and stood up.

"Fine by me," I grumbled.

She approached me, and her eyes raked me from head to toe. "You honestly believe she has it in her?"

Sinjin tightened his hold around me. "Without a doubt," he said sternly. "And I do not recall asking you for your opinion."

Bella looked at me, her jaw tight. "Let's see if you truly are such a powerful witch. All you need to do is focus within yourself and draw your sister beast to the forefront. She will choose you."

I glanced at her and then at Sinjin before my mouth dropped open. "What does that even mean?"

Sinjin looked down at me, a sweet smile on his beautiful face. "Your magic works only if you concentrate on it, love. You must guide your power, tell it what you expect of it."

"Okay," I said, still not sure what I was doing. Did everything have to be so esoteric where magic was concerned?

"Close your eyes," Bella snapped and I obeyed. "Now imagine a field full of animals, as many as you possibly can."

I exhaled as I debated about inquiring whether I should be selective in my imagining the animals. But deciding Bella probably wouldn't react nicely, I just went with my gut and imagined an enormous pasture, like what you'd see in the farmlands of the Midwest. Then I pictured an elephant dropping from the sky and landing with a thud on the ground. He wasn't hurt, though. The next animal up was a hyena, who landed a few paces behind the elephant, followed by a yak and then a dog that looked like Lassie.

"Are you done?" Bella insisted.

I clenched my eyes even more tightly closed and realized I only had a dozen or so animals in my pasture. "How many do I need?"

Bella grumbled something that I couldn't make out. But she didn't say anything else so I continued imagining animals dropping from the sky until it looked like I had the best-ever petting zoo.

"K," I said, finally satisfied.

"Now, without losing your focus, tell the animals to come forth and claim you."

"Okay," I whispered and imagined myself walking into the pasture. Then I cleared my throat and said in my best authoritative voice: *Please come and claim me.*

And nothing happened. So I said it again. Still nothing.

"Um, nothing's happening," I said aloud, being sure to keep my eyes shut.

"It may take a few moments, but eventually, one will," Bella responded.

I shut my eyes even more tightly and focused on the animals that were now surrounding me—an elephant, tiger, all sorts of birds, an alligator, various rodents, anything I could think of. Then I said to myself: *Please select me. Whoever you are, please select me.*

Then a funny thing happened. An elephant and a monkey stepped forward at the same time, followed by a puma and coyote, as well as a red-tailed hawk that soared overhead. "Um," I started.

"What?" Bella snapped.

"What is bothering you, poppet?" Sinjin whispered.

"What do I do if more than one animal comes forward?" I asked, still keeping my eyes clamped shut, afraid the animals might disperse if I opened them.

"There can't be more than one," Bella said, her tone dismissive and impatient. "There will be only one."

I looked at the animals that were now circling me. Yeah, there was definitely more than just one. "Um, are you sure?"

"Just choose one!" Bella snapped.

I looked around me again. The elephant sidled somewhat closer but, figuring an elephant would do a number on Sinjin's living room, I turned to the monkey. After Bella's little sexy-lioness show, however, the last thing I wanted to do was show up as a freaking chimpanzee or baboon. I continued until my eyes rested on an animal that would certainly give Bella's lioness a run for her money. A tigress.

And then a feeling of lightness descended on me—as if my soul were floating to the very top of my head. I opened my eyes and found myself on all fours. I glanced down and noticed the stripes of the tiger coloring my paws, which were in a word . . . huge. So this could only mean . . . I'd done it! Somehow, and I had no idea how, I just managed to magick myself into a tigress.

Holy crap! I am a witch!

And that was when I realized for certain that I was something more than I'd ever thought I was or could be. It wasn't really so much that I'd turned myself from human girl into wild cat; more that I'd been able to control whatever power existed within me to actually be able to do something so completely . . . impossible. At that moment I felt a huge outpouring of emotion toward Sinjin. He'd been right all along—I was far more than I thought I was and it was because of him that I'd been able to cultivate my abilities, to hone my powers. Sinjin was my teacher, my mentor, and what was more, he had never stopped believing in me. Even when I doubted myself.

You will never doubt yourself again, Jolie Wilkins, I thought firmly.

Taking a resolute step forward, I focused on my surroundings. Everything appeared almost colorless, and distorted—as if I were looking through a bottle. I looked up at Sinjin and felt my heartbeat increase. He was just as stunning as always, but his eyes were bright red. The way he shifted looked as if he were moving a million miles a second, and strangely enough I could see every fraction of his movement. It wasn't just a blur.

I took another few steps, feeling wobbly on my new legs. I glanced up at Sinjin again and tried to say something, which only came out as a growl. He approached me, kneeling until we were eye level.

"You are stunning, love," he whispered.

At the word *love,* I growled at him again and he chuckled, as if he understood. Then, just as quickly as the bizarre sense of light-headedness had overcome me, it started again. I shook my head and found myself suddenly lying in Sinjin's arms. I glanced down and felt my cheeks flush as I realized I was completely naked, just as Bella had been.

"She is a tigress, as I knew she would be," Sinjin announced to the room, pulling me closer. Apparently realizing I wasn't as comfortable as Bella with public shows of nudity, he tore off his shirt and slid it over my head and arms. It fit me like a dress. And of course I didn't miss the display of his incredibly muscled chest, which caused a hiccup in my heart rate.

"Very good," Bella said in a hurried, dismissive sort of way. "I imagine we will be in touch."

He smiled at her courteously and kissed the top of my head. She stormed out of the room. Judging by the fact that I heard the front door slam shut behind her only moments later, I had to imagine she'd seen herself out.

"You share an unusual friendship," I started.

He nodded. "Truly we are not friends."

"Then why?"

"She owes me," he interrupted. "Speak no more of her, poppet. I am much more interested in you."

I imagined this was his line to move us into the bedroom. I smiled up at him. "Interested in me?"

"You had a multitude of animals to choose from, you said?" he asked. I felt my hopes deflate. I mean, how hard was it for a girl to get a little action?

"Yeah, I think so."

"Can you demonstrate?"

I took a deep breath and figured there was no point in arguing with him. Besides, I *was* curious as to whether or not I could become another creature. I closed my eyes and was surprised to find it took no time at all for all the animals to assemble around me again. This time my attention centered on an eagle, perched in a nearby tree. I focused on the gallant raptor and the same feeling of light-headedness began to fill me. Then, in the span of a blink, I was in Sinjin's kitchen, standing on the counter and glancing down at the room while an array of colors reflected back at me. The brightness of the colors astounded me—they were like nothing I'd ever seen before. I guess it made sense because a bird's vision included a much broader spectrum of colors than a human's.

I heard Sinjin chuckling but couldn't seem to focus on him and realized my eyes were now on the sides of my head. I hopped around, turning my head in order to see him. The scratching of my talons against his granite countertops scraped in my ears and I had to hope he wouldn't be concerned about me damaging them. When I turned my eagle head, I could see him out of the corner of my eye. He was entirely black, like a shadow.

"Can you fly, poppet?"

I lifted my arms—er, wings—and flapped a few times before kicking off with my legs to find myself airborne. But I never had the chance to fully experience the rush of flying, because seconds later the dizziness from before returned. My heartbeat escalated at the thought that I was midair and resuming my human body. I didn't have much time to worry, though, because the next thing I knew, I was falling.

"Sinjin!" I screamed out and felt the air stirring beneath me as Sinjin materialized just in time to catch me in his large arms. I glanced down at myself, to find I was naked again. When I looked up at Sinjin, he was grinning from ear to ear.

"You do not realize the immensity of the gift you have," he said softly, his eyes running down my naked body as his fangs began to lengthen.

"Gift?" I asked with a smile, loving the expression of pride in his eyes. "Well, one thing I can say is I'm pretty convinced that I'm a witch."

He chuckled deeply, heartily. "You are much more than a witch, my pet."

"More than a witch?"

He nodded. "I have never known of any witch or warlock with the power to transform into more than one creature, poppet." He shook his head in apparent surprise. "You are an anomaly."

An anomaly? I wasn't sure what to make of it. I was having enough trouble just coming to terms with being something super-human. After everyone else decided I was a witch, I sort of figured there must have been some truth to it. But to be something more than a witch? I didn't even know what that meant, or could possibly mean . . .

THREE

The next evening, I found myself sitting on my couch, bobbing my leg anxiously as I tried to watch television. I actually had no idea what program was on because my mind was wholly absorbed by Sinjin. We planned to have dinner in at my place (well, dinner for me, anyway) and a nice, relaxed, romantic evening with just the two of us. The night before had been anything but relaxing, what with the Bella drama, so Sinjin had promised to make it up to me tonight.

Speaking of my last meeting with Sinjin, I still didn't quite know what to make of everything. Really, for the first time since Sinjin entered my life, I found myself concerned about what was becoming of me. I felt different down to my very core. Yes, I looked different because I was paying more attention to my outward appearance, but the changes within me were much more significant. I was not the same woman today that I had been two months ago. And truth be told, I was struggling with those changes, not the least of which was my ability to morph into two animals. I had no clue what had made that at all possible. How could I, Jolie Wilkins, now turn myself into a tiger and an eagle?

My mind had been stretching in order to make room for the reality of vampires, witches, and warlocks. It only continued to stretch with the sure knowledge that I was included in this much esteemed company. Yet I felt as though I'd just about reached my limit after the events of last night. It was almost as if my mind refused to accept any more. What if I *had* completely lost my mind and was now living in some parallel universe, fueled purely by my imagination? What if Sinjin and Rand were entirely made up? In that case, maybe the lion, tiger, and eagle transmogrifications were hallucinations too? I mean, that would make a hell of a lot more sense than actually accepting the fact that I was still a perfectly sane woman.

I glanced up at the clock on my wall and noticed it was seven p.m. Sinjin wouldn't be arriving for at least another thirty minutes. Out the window the sun was on her way out, bathing the world in a darkish rose hue. I never wanted the sun to go down faster than I did now. Although I didn't want to admit it, and definitely wasn't comfortable with it, the truth was that I yearned for Sinjin constantly. Whenever I wasn't with him, he was the only thing on my mind.

I smiled when I remembered last night—how Sinjin had made love to me repeatedly, how tender he'd been and attentive. He said more than once how terrible he felt about the whole Bella situation and how I had become the most important woman in his life. No one else mattered to him. Well, if Sinjin was just the creation of my befuddled mind, I'd done a damn good job, that was for sure.

My inner monologue was interrupted by a knock on the door. Puzzled, I glanced at the clock again and realized only ten minutes had elapsed. Looking out my window, I realized dusk had arrived, although it still seemed too light for Sinjin. But apparently I was wrong.

I stood up and glanced down at my skintight jeans and low-cut black, stretch T-shirt, imagining Sinjin would appreciate my cleavage spilling over the top. I ran my tongue across my teeth to ensure that my pink NARS lip gloss hadn't smudged and then fluffed my hair a few times. Finally, I felt a smile begin as I opened my front door.

And instantly my smile vanished.

My first instinct was to slam the door shut, but he was too quick and, instead, threw all his weight into the door, forcing it open. It was like time stood still as I tried to sidestep him, hoping I could make it through my kitchen to the back door, but he seemed to read my mind. As soon as I made a move for it, he thrust himself forward and knocked me on my butt. I squealed as I hit the ground, but immediately tried to stand up. He was too fast for me. In a split second, he slammed the door shut and threw his body back on me, forcing me down to the floor.

Bella's spell hadn't worked. Or maybe Rand's magic had been stronger, and he'd broken her charm.

"Get the hell off me!" I screamed as I pushed against him, but he was way too solid. He pinned my hands down on either side of my head. At his touch, that now familiar sense of electricity coursed through me and those ridiculous feelings of warmth began to well up inside me.

You are a freaking idiot, Jolie Wilkins! I chided myself. *This asshole is probably going to rape you and then kill you and all you can think about is his great energy and how he feels familiar!*

At the realization that I couldn't fight him, that I was now in serious trouble, I started screaming. He went for my mouth and tried to cover it with his hand but I threw my head left then right, screaming louder in the vain hope my neighbors would hear me.

"Jolie!" he yelled as he grabbed both of my cheeks with one large hand. "It's no use—I've soundproofed your house!"

I stopped screaming and tried to struggle from his massive hand, but of course got nowhere. Meanwhile, a continuous flow of terror was contaminating my insides at the realization that no one could hear me. "What the hell do you mean you soundproofed my house?" I finally demanded in a raw voice.

"Magic," he answered in a matter-of-fact sort of way. He breathed out a sigh of relief, probably because I was no longer thrashing against him or screaming.

Neither of us said anything for a few seconds. We just stared at each other as we both tried to get our breathing under control. Rand was the first to speak.

"I'm not here to hurt you."

I shook my head and laughed acidly. "I don't believe a word you say." And that was when it occurred to me. If I could just stall him long enough, Sinjin would arrive and there would be hell to pay. I also considered morphing into a tiger and mauling the shit out of him—but then I remembered that whole nudity bit once I returned to normal, and that part didn't sit so well with me.

"What do you want?" I demanded.

He swallowed hard. I couldn't help but notice how incredibly handsome he was with his chocolate-brown hair, now completely mussed, and his clothes all askew and rumpled. Well, gorgeous warlock or not, he remained dangerous. And that's what I had to keep in mind.

"Nothing could keep me from you."

"What?" I asked, gulping down the anxiety at the very thought that all this time, he could get to me, Bella's spell be damned. "How is that even possible?"

"It's a long story," he started and then sighed deeply. "And it's the reason why I've come here. Did you receive my package?"

I glared at him but nodded. "Yes, I received it."

"And did you watch the whole thing?"

"Yes but that doesn't mean I believed a word of it."

He sighed again, seemingly frustrated. "There's so much more I need to tell you, so much to explain to you, so you understand."

But I shook my head, not wanting to hear another word of his "drivel," as Sinjin had termed it. Then it suddenly occurred to me that I'd be putting Sinjin in a dangerous situation. I mean, he'd have no idea Rand was here or what magical abilities Rand had up his sleeve.

I would never forgive myself if something happened to Sinjin on my account. "I don't want to hear another lie from you," I spat back. "I want you to leave."

He shook his head and I could see his jaw was tight. "We can do this the easy way or the hard way. I'm leaving the choice up to you."

Sighing, I figured it was probably easier to persuade warlocks with honey than with vinegar. "What's the easy way?"

He shrugged. "We sit down, like civilized people, and you listen to what I have to say."

"So, after I listen to you, you'll leave?"

He took a deep breath and there was something in his eyes that looked hurt, painfully so. Or maybe I was just imagining it. "Yes."

I glanced at the clock and realized it was now seven thirty. It was also completely dark outside. Sinjin should be arriving any minute . . . "I . . . I have plans tonight but how about tomorrow?"

"Plans?" Rand's eyes narrowed, as he seemed to consider my offer. "And how can I be sure you'll actually show up tomorrow? You haven't exactly been accommodating thus far."

"Well, you know where I live so it's not like you won't be able to hunt me down." I frowned. "Something you've already proven you can do."

He seemed okay with a rain check and stood up, extending his hand to me as he did so, but I ignored it, pushing myself up and off the floor, dusting my jeans. I wasn't sure why, but for some reason I no longer felt afraid of him. It was almost as if his consenting to come back tomorrow negated all of my dread. It was weird and probably stupid, to say the least.

"What is this?" he demanded. Before I could stop him, he brushed my hair away from my neck, and his features contorted with anger when he saw Sinjin's teeth marks.

"That fucking bastard!" Rand yelled, his hands fisting at his sides. He turned around and I could see the rage in the tightness of his shoulders. Before I could even blink, he smashed his fist into my door.

"What is wrong with you?" I yelled, taking a few steps back, suddenly afraid again. Nothing like a pissed-off man unable to control his temper to jar me back to my senses. I mean, I knew he was a dangerous warlock. It shouldn't have taken an act of what appeared to be jealousy, strangely enough, to assure me of that.

He turned to face me and there was fury in his dark brown eyes, as well as a certain hollowness and pain. "I should never have let it progress this far," he said, mostly to himself. Then, before I could guess what would happen next, he lunged for me and grabbed my arm, pulling me toward the door.

"Let go of me!" I screamed, pulling against him.

"You're coming with me, Jolie," he said in a voice that brooked no argument. "It's for your own good."

I tried to extricate myself from him, but fighting him was useless. He was built like a mountain lion—sleek, yes, but also incredibly strong. "I'm not going anywhere with you!"

He instantly stopped dragging me and, instead, turned to face me. His expression was completely unreadable, but he didn't let go of my arm. "You will never forgive Sinjin for what he's done to you."

"What are you talking about?" I yelled as I struggled against him again, trying to pull my arm from his viselike grip. He simply held me tighter. "You're hurting me!"

He let go of me then, as if I'd bitten him. I lost my balance as I tripped over my ridiculous wedge sandals and crumbled into a clumsy heap on the floor.

"This was never meant to happen, Jolie," Rand said as he approached me again, standing above me. I knew I wouldn't get far if I tried to bolt, so I stayed put.

"What was never meant to happen?"

He looked around himself and waved his hands as if to include everything—us, my house, my neighborhood, the whole world. "It was always you and me."

"Sinjin—"

"Sinjin never had a claim on you!" he interrupted. Then he shook his head as if this whole thing were a big misunderstanding and a damn shame at that.

"You aren't making any sense," I said, my voice softer as I realized I was dealing with someone who wasn't playing with a full deck. "There's nothing between you and me and there never was. I don't even know you!"

He shook his head and laughed but it was not a happy sound. "That's where you're wrong, Jolie. You and I have known each other for years. I taught you everything you know."

"But—" I started, shaking my head as I tried to comprehend his statement.

"The life you're leading now is a farce—it's all because that bastard Sinjin wanted you for himself and he knew the only way he'd have a chance in hell of wooing you away from me was to make contact with you first."

"That doesn't even make any sense!" I yelled at him again and stood up, wrapping my arms around myself protectively. "Look, I don't know who the hell you are . . ."

Then he was in front of me, grabbing my shoulders and holding me still. I could feel his breath fanning the naked skin of my chest and I closed my eyes. "Yes, you do, Jolie," he said softly, whispering as my breathing lengthened. There was just something so familiar about him, something that made me want to yield to him.

Resist the feelings, Jolie! I yelled at myself. *It's nothing but his warlock magic trying to charm you, making you feel like you've known him forever!*

It can't be. We're close—I can feel it in my blood, in the center of my being.

You haven't even known him two weeks!

Then why do I feel like this? I argued. *I know this man. I've known him for a long time. I can feel it. And you can't deny it either.*

"It's impossible," I said out loud and shook my head, opening my eyes and focusing on the dark chocolate pools of his.

"What's impossible?" Rand asked, his eyes searching, pleading.

"I. Don't. Know. You."

He took a deep breath and shook his head, even as I fought the need to believe everything he said. "You know me—deep down, I know you do."

But I refused to give into the part of me that wanted to believe him. Instead, I forced myself to consider how absurd the whole thing was. I had only just met him when he walked into my store. He and I meant nothing to each other; we weren't even acquaintances. "You must have me confused with someone else."

"No," he said, anger and frustration returning to his voice. He shook his head adamantly. "I have known you intimately, Jolie, I've known you like no other man ever could."

I swallowed hard. I knew he meant in more ways than just sexually, but it was the sexual connotation that made me blush right down to my feet. I dropped my gaze to my shaking hands, trying to figure out my next course of action, inventing a plan of escape.

"Look at me," he said, and I wasn't sure why, but I acquiesced. When I did, I felt the urge to believe him grow stronger. I felt that same sense of familiarity welling up inside me all over again.

"Stop doing that," I whispered, afraid because I could feel myself succumbing to the power he wielded over me. As strange as it sounded and as much as I didn't want to admit it, there was still something in me that needed to believe him, and to accept him.

"Doing what?"

"Making me feel things that aren't real."

He chuckled then, heartily. "It is real, Jolie. Whatever you're feeling for me is real."

"No, it isn't." I paused, taking a deep breath. "It's your magic."

He pulled me closer to him, and I was surprised at my lack of resistance. It was the same as it had been when he came to my store—as if I dissolved into mush in his hands. "No it's not my magic—it's the connection between us."

I closed my eyes and shook my head, feeling as if everything I knew, my entire world, was now under siege again. "I met you only a week or two ago," I started, reminding myself more than him.

"Jolie, I walked into your store two years ago and I've loved you ever since."

I felt my eyes open wide as I tried to make sense of his words. "Loved me?" I repeated, shocked.

He nodded and smiled almost shyly. My entire body began to quake from the inside out, to shake with the need to touch him, kiss him. I forced the feelings down, straining to recognize them for what they were—the spell of a master magician and nothing more.

"You have been the only woman in my life and you will continue to be the only woman I could ever love."

And that was all it took— just a brief reminder of a similar sentiment from Sinjin—to remind me that Rand was not the one I was meant to be with, that everything he was telling me was a lie. I loved Sinjin, that's all there was to it. "You need to leave," I said frigidly.

"Don't fight this, Jolie." He looked into my eyes, and I couldn't pull my gaze away. "God, you are so beautiful," he said and I felt my heart flutter at his words. "You have no idea how worried I've been about you, how much I've missed you."

Then his lips were on mine and I was shocked and disgusted with myself when I did nothing to fight him. In fact, I welcomed his lips and encouraged his tongue to find entrance into my mouth. He ran his hands through my hair and I felt myself melt against him.

"My, my! Such a happy little couple."

I heard Sinjin's voice. I pulled away from Rand and turned to Sinjin in the doorway, but he didn't seem upset in the least. Rather, he appeared merely entertained. He was wearing that smirky smile, but when I looked at his eyes I realized he was livid.

"Sinjin. I . . . I don't know what happened," I started, realizing how completely horrible this situation looked. He'd basically just walked in on me kissing another man.

He faced me, shaking his head. "Do not apologize, little poppet. The warlock's coercive powers were too much for you to fend off."

I glanced at Rand and didn't know what to think. Had it been his magic all along that caused me to feel and act this way? Maybe, but there was definitely something inside me that felt as if I were right where I needed to be—in his arms. I almost felt as if I'd come home.

"Come," Sinjin said to me. Still in a fog of confused emotions, I pulled away from Rand and walked closer to Sinjin, all the while fighting the need to return to Rand's arms. Sinjin grabbed me and pulled me close to his chest, never dropping his eyes from Rand's. "She is mine, Balfour. The sooner you realize that, the better." Then he smiled, his eyes narrow. "You have been spurned."

Rand was fuming—I could see it in the red of his cheeks, his shallow breathing, his chest rising and falling. "You've gone too far this time, Sinjin," he managed to spit out. Then he faced me. "Step away from him, Jolie."

I glanced at Sinjin as though I were seeking his permission, or at the least, to get a clue of what was happening. He merely smiled down at me and nodded, pushing me slightly from him. "Randall . . ."

But he never finished his sentence. Instead, I watched, horrified, as Rand lunged for him and threw him to the ground. Rand pulled his arm back and pummeled Sinjin's face as the vampire held up his arms to protect himself. In a split second, Sinjin disappeared from below Rand and reappeared behind him. But Rand was prepared, seeming to fly off his feet, pivoting around. He ducked in time to miss Sinjin's blow and delivered his own series of jabs into Sinjin's stomach. All in all, it seemed as if they were pretty evenly matched.

"Stop!" I screamed and, not even thinking, rushed over to the two of them. I threw myself onto Rand's back, toppling over a table just beside the door in the process. But I wasn't concerned. Instead, all my distress was reserved for the fight that was in the process of blowing up between the two men. Grabbing Rand's forearms, I screamed again. "Stop it!"

Rand merely shook me off and dived for Sinjin. "You will pay for what you've done, bastard!" Rand yelled. The vampire chuckled and sidestepped him, giving me the opportunity to wedge myself between the two of them.

"I love him!" I screamed at Rand, not even realizing what I was saying or what I was admitting in front of Sinjin. I'd promised myself I wouldn't (well, not until he admitted it to me first). But the time for regrets was over. "Whatever you think we share isn't real!" I continued, tears flooding my eyes.

Rand stood stock-still, his shallow breathing betraying his exhaustion. But I couldn't look away from his face. He was devastated. He continued staring at me, pain and betrayal in his eyes. But I didn't care. If his relentless hunt for me was based on unrequited love, I needed to nip it in the bud . . . now.

"If you truly care about me, then you'll leave us alone!" I screamed again, tears streaming down my face. "Because I love Sinjin."

"Jolie," he started, taking a step toward me.

I held him back with my hand. "No," I said, my voice cracking with the effort. "Whatever you think we have, it's nothing more than a delusion."

"Just listen to me," he said.

I shook my head. "I have nothing more to say to you."

He took a deep breath and ran his fingers through his hair as he shook his head but said nothing more. He walked past me and hesitated only momentarily. Once he approached Sinjin, though, he stopped and faced him with hatred flashing from his eyes.

"This isn't over, Sinclair," he said. "I will never stop until she understands what you did to her."

Smiling, Sinjin threw his arm around my shoulder and pulled me close to him, kissing the top of my head. Rand's lips were tight as he turned around and disappeared out my front door. For some strange reason, and I wasn't sure why, there was something within me that felt numb, something hollow and sad, that I hadn't felt before.

I pulled away from Sinjin, my head ready to explode, there were so many thoughts and questions running through it. I immediately noticed that any damage Rand might have inflicted on him had already healed.

"What was he talking about?" I demanded.

Sinjin shook his head. "The nonsensical ravings of a madman."

I didn't say anything right away but, somehow, I knew he was lying to me.

Sinjin has no reason to lie to you, Jolie, part of me argued. *Rand has just completely lost his mind and must think you're someone else. Or he's just trying to manipulate you into believing there's something between you.*

That may be, my other half replied, *but I also think Sinjin's holding out—that he knows more than he's letting on. He just makes everything seem so simple and I know well enough that that is never the case.*

"Did I meet Rand . . . before? Like, a long time ago?"

Sinjin faced me with a smile. "Poppet, that is a question only you can answer. I know of no affiliation between you and the warlock."

I shook my head, trying to understand how any of this made sense, trying to fill in the pieces. "I met him in my store not long ago, like I told you."

"Then you have your answer."

"But why does he seem to think . . ."

"He is mad, love," he said simply. "If you remembered the moment you met him accurately and it truly was only a week or two ago, as you claim, then that can only be the truth, correct?"

I nodded, relieved that it made lots more sense to just trust Sinjin. That part of me that insisted I could only have known Rand for a matter of days had to be right. I mean, what more could I go on? It's not like I could remember meeting Rand earlier. The whole thing was completely absurd.

I faced him with a smile and nodded. "Yes, you're right."

"Poppet," he started and approached me with a twinkle in his eyes.

"Yes?" I responded.

"Did you mean what you said?"

I gulped hard, realizing he was referring to when I basically yelled at Rand that I was in love with Sinjin. Well, no use in denying it now. The cat was already way out of the bag. I dropped my eyes to the ground and felt my cheeks flush. "Yes."

Instantly, he was before me, tilting my chin up so I could gaze into his face. There was a passion in his eyes I'd never seen before. He just stared at me for a few seconds, and when he spoke his voice was deadly serious. "You do not know how I have yearned to hear those words."

FOUR

My eyes flew open, my heartbeat pounding away in my chest. I took a deep breath and tried to calm myself, trying to persuade myself that whatever nightmare I'd just awoken from was just that—a nightmare, nothing more. Staring at the dark ceiling of my bedroom, I realized night was still upon me. I turned my head to the side, the clock on my bedside table glowing two thirty in the morning. Sitting up, I rubbed my eyes. Somehow I just couldn't shake off the feeling of dread instigated by the dream—it was still eerily haunting me.

Jolie, it was just a dream, something you completely made up in that ridiculous head of yours! I tried to reassure myself. But it was one of those nightmares where you can't really stop thinking about it—despite knowing that you're safely ensconced in your own bed, in your own house, and whatever evils your brain created aren't real and can't hurt you.

This nightmare wasn't so much about the visuals, though, as the feelings it drummed up within me—anxiety, hopelessness, dread . . . familiarity. It was as if I'd seen it all before, that uncanny déjà vu everyone experiences sometime in his or her life. The strangest part about the whole thing, though, was that although the images of the nightmare were macabre, they meant nothing to me. I lay back down again and closed my

eyes, trying to go back to sleep, but all I could focus on were the visions that had just faded— from a nightmare that made no sense at all . . . So why couldn't I shake it?

The dream began with scenes of open land that was devastated and barren, like a bomb had gone off. But the lumps on the ground were what grabbed my attention. They were people lying facedown in muck, people who were also very much dead. Almost as quickly as the vision upset me, it receded into the distance of my subconscious and another one replaced it. This dreamscape centered on a throne that was vacant. A scepter and a crown stood at either side of a golden chair. Then, just like that, the image of the chair was ripped away, replaced by a battle scene. I saw creatures I knew—witches, warlocks, and vampires—as well as others that I didn't recognize. They all displayed extraordinary powers as they battled one another, fighting to the death. The term *Lurkers* entered my mind, and seemed to eat through my body like cancer. Just as quickly as the image of the combative creatures vanished from my unconscious mind, the image of the throne returned. This time, however, the crown and the scepter began melting into the base of the golden chair. And that's what woke me up, now a frantic mess in a cold sweat.

    As I lay in my bed and coaxed my mind to rest—to ignore the meaningless dreamscapes—I started to feel an overwhelming sense of exhaustion, almost of nausea. What did it mean that the word *Lurkers* was in my dream? I remembered Sinjin telling me about the Lurkers, how Bella had cast that spell to learn what they were up to. I shook the feelings of dread aside. It was merely my subconscious playing tricks on me, bringing to light subjects from my conscious mind. Still, mind trick or not, I suddenly didn't want to be alone. I was cross with myself for telling Sinjin I needed to be alone tonight, that I had to sleep. Really, that was never the truth. Instead, I'd been so bothered by his exchange with Rand, I felt I needed some "me-time" away from the imposing, larger-than-life vampire.

Yes, I loved Sinjin, but I couldn't deny that there was something within me that didn't entirely believe him, not 100 percent, anyway. So, seeking some elucidation, I opted for a night on my own. I hoped that with some time to think about everything that had happened, I could figure out what to make of the whole ordeal. Well, that was then. Now I would have gladly traded in the me-time for some Sinjin-time. I just felt strangely feeble—like an incredibly rapid illness had started consuming me, draining me of strength. Of course, that was ludicrous—it wasn't like dreams could cause illness.

I tossed and turned for a few more minutes, unable to get comfortable. After another ten minutes, during which I counted 150 sheep, 70 horses, 54 chickens, and 20 rabbits, I decided to give up. I sat up and took a deep breath, fighting the realization that I truly wasn't well. The more I fought it, however, the more I knew I had just contracted a case of the most contagious fl u known to man. I brought the top of my hand to my forehead and checked my temperature the old-fashioned way.

I was definitely feverish.

Then, deciding not to rely on such a non-scientific test, I pushed the bedclothes aside and forced myself up. Instantly, I felt light-headed and almost dazed. I managed to make it to my bathroom where I turned on the light and groped inside my top drawer for the thermometer. I stuck it in my mouth and waited. When it beeped its signal, I pulled it out and read it. I was running a temperature of 104.

"What?" I asked out loud. I shook it, thinking there must have been something wrong with the thermometer, and put it back under my tongue. A minute later it beeped again, revealing the same result. I was on fire!

Now really nervous, I threw open my medicine cabinet and searched for the Tylenol. I swiftly downed two of the gel caps and glanced in the mirror, noting how pale my skin looked and damp my hairline was—from sweat.

"What is wrong with me?" I asked my reflection. As I hobbled back to bed, I felt pathetically feeble and frail. I sort of collapsed on top of it and managed to wrap the duvet cover over me, taco-style. That was when I knew something was seriously wrong. I'd never had a cold or a flu develop so quickly. What if I'd picked up a strange infection like *E. coli* or something equally unpleasant? What if I had flesh-eating bacteria? I felt my stomach suddenly recoiling at the thought and I had to wonder if the bacteria hadn't already invaded, devouring my stomach lining.

I reached for the phone beside my bed and dialed Sinjin's number.

"Poppet," he answered on the first ring. "Why are you awake at this hour? I thought you needed your rest?" His tone was jovial, as if he was delighted to hear my voice.

"Something's wrong with me, Sinjin," I said as I shivered despite myself. "I think I have that flesh-eating bacteria."

"Wrong with you?" he repeated, any joy now completely absent from his tone. "Flesh-eating bacteria?"

"Yes, I feel incredibly sick and weak."

"I will be there momentarily," he said and, before I could respond, he hung up. I placed the phone on the cradle and huddled in the fetal position, trying to will myself warm, but chills were now running up and down my body.

No more than five minutes passed between the time I got off the phone with Sinjin and his arrival at my house. I heard him try the front door and remembered I'd locked it. Then I heard his footsteps as he walked around the house, eventually finding his way to my bedroom window. I sat up and took a deep breath, unsure of how I would stand up and walk over to the window to let him in. I hobbled a few steps but suddenly felt light-headed, seeing stars orbiting around me. Leaning and off balance, I started to succumb to what I assumed was a faint and caught myself on my boudoir chair in the corner of the room.

At the sound of shattered glass, I didn't need to glance up to know Sinjin had just arrived. Within an instant, he was beside me, heaving me into his arms as he crunched on the glass underfoot. I couldn't find it within me to complain about my smashed bedroom window. I was just too tired, too sick to care.

"What is the matter, poppet?" he asked with visible concern. "What is wrong with you?"

I nestled my head against his broad chest and closed my eyes for a moment, relishing the fact that he was here, that he would take care of me. "I don't know," I whispered. "I just remember this weird dream and then, I felt so weak and so . . . so sick."

He lay me down on my bed and I shivered as soon as he removed his hands. Strangely enough, considering how cold he was, I felt warmer in his arms. He wrapped the duvet around me and sat down close to me, stroking my hair like a mother would her sick child.

"Describe the dream."

I closed my eyes, wanting only to sleep off my feelings of exhaustion and weariness. But Sinjin tapped my shoulder as if to remind me that I hadn't answered him. I yawned and tried to remember the dream again. "It was just a bunch of images," I started. "The first was a battlefield of dead bodies. Then there was an empty throne with a scepter and a crown." I glanced up at him and saw him swallow hard. It was almost as if he could see the very scenes I was describing. Something in his eyes hinted at familiarity; he didn't seem shocked or surprised.

"Go on," he prodded.

"I remember the word *Lurkers* repeating over and over again through my head." I was quiet for a second or two as scenes from the dream returned anew. "But it wasn't even my voice in my head that was saying the word," I said, amazed by the sudden realization. "I think it was a man's voice that kept repeating 'Lurkers.' It was as if someone else sent the dream to me."

"And then what happened, poppet?" Sinjin asked, his tone purposeful, his eyes narrowed on me.

I shook my head, still fixated on the idea that the dream seemed forced—as if it hadn't really been mine. "Then seconds after I woke up, I had a fever and started feeling awful."

"I see." He glanced down at me with a fake smile, as if he was trying to hide what was in his eyes—could it be fear? "Perhaps you have caught the flu?"

I shook my head, refusing to believe that my current condition had anything to do with a virus. At this point, I'd also ruled out the flesh-eating bacteria. No, this was somehow connected to my nightmare. I was certain of it. "Sinjin, what does this mean?"

He shook his head, crossing his arms against his chest as he did so. "I do not know, love." But something in his expression screamed the opposite. After a few seconds of silence, he said, "Poppet, I think we should call Isabella."

"Bella?" I asked, as my stomach dropped to my feet. I felt like vomiting now more than ever before. The last thing I wanted to do was deal with that snobby bitch again, especially when I wasn't feeling my normal, patient, good-natured self.

He nodded and stood up, fishing his iPhone from his pocket. "I want her to . . . examine you."

I tried to sit up but found I wasn't strong enough. "Examine me?" I took a deep breath, suddenly finding it difficult to inhale as I was seized with a fit of coughing. Once I'd gotten myself under control again, I said, "I don't understand."

But he said nothing more as I watched him dial Bella on his cell phone. Then he turned his back on me as if he didn't want me to overhear their conversation. A few seconds later, he clicked off his phone, sliding it back into his pocket as he turned to face me with an artificial smile.

"Why are you acting so weird?" I demanded.

"Weird, poppet?"

"My dream didn't seem to surprise you at all."

He shook his head and sat down beside me, rubbing my shoulder as he gave me a reassuring smile. "It must be your fever speaking, love. I have no knowledge of your dream."

I figured it was useless to argue, especially when I was feeling so crappy. "Why does Bella have to come over?" I asked, turning to something else that aggravated me.

He sighed. "I want to be certain there is not more to this sudden illness of yours than meets the eye."

"Do you think it's magic-related, then?" I asked, feeling the tentacles of a headache starting between my eyes. I closed my eyes and purposefully willed the headache to go away. It surprised me when the pain began to fade away into nothing.

"Perhaps," he said simply before facing me again, compassion in his ice-blue gaze. "Poppet, you need to rest and conserve your strength to overcome this bug. Please no more questions."

I wanted to argue with him, to demand an explanation as to how and why he thought magic was involved, but he was correct, I did need to conserve my strength. I was now even more exhausted than before. It was as if the willpower to send my headache packing had zapped me of any remaining energy I possessed.

I closed my eyes and tried to sleep, but was unsuccessful. Instead, I listened to the sound of Sinjin cleaning up the broken glass from the window, and then his footsteps as he paced back and forth, obviously distressed by my condition. I found myself zoning out with the rhythm of his footfalls against my wood floor. I wondered why there were times when he didn't make a sound, and could walk up behind me without me ever hearing him. Yet at other times, he made as much sound as a regular person.

The next thing I knew, Sinjin was at my bedside with Bella. I didn't recall the sound of her knocking on my door, nor had I heard him leaving my room to let her in. So either I'd fallen asleep for a few seconds, or my fever was accompanied by delirium.

"What is wrong with her?" Bella demanded caustically, eyeing me with disinterest. I didn't get a good look at her but what I saw was enough. She was dressed in skintight black pants and a magenta sweater with a deeply plunging neckline. I bet this woman couldn't be casual if she tried.

I heard Sinjin inhale deeply before he told her, "I am not certain. However, I believe it to be a magical attack."

"A magical attack?" she repeated in an abrasive tone. "Who would possibly want to attack her? No one knows about her anyway." She sounded dismissive, not to mention irritated that someone would bother about me—since she saw me as just a nobody.

"I refuse to discuss the specifics with you, Isabella. Please use your powers to detect what has happened to her."

There was silence for a few seconds, but I could feel the tension in the room. It didn't take a genius to realize that Bella not only was unaccustomed to being spoken to in such a way, but really didn't like it. "I am not at your beck and call, Sinjin," she said flatly.

"You know why you are here," he countered. By the sound of his voice, he was just as irritated as she was.

"I understand we have an agreement, but—"

"Enough!" His angry tone caused my heart to race for a few seconds, and I felt a rush of pain in my head. The headache I'd just willed away moments before had returned with a vengeance.

"Put her on her back," Bella said in an aggravated voice.

I felt Sinjin's hands on either of my shoulders, and he smiled down at me almost apologetically as he gently rolled me from my side to my back. Then he pulled away and I was faced with Bella's beautiful but fuming countenance. She narrowed her eyes as she looked down at me and offered no form of a greeting. Instead, she held out her hands, palms above me, and closed her eyes. Her lips twitched as she seemed to recite some sort of chant in her head. But it was the space between her hands that had me enthralled as a light began to build between them. It was purplish and then began to morph into what resembled smoke, circling between her palms. She opened her eyes and brought her hands to my face, touching her fingers to my temples. At her touch, the smallest spark of energy— a gentle drumming that fizzed against my skin—ran through me. I could see the purplish smoke light cycling around my head now, right before my eyes. I glanced at Bella and noticed her eyes were shut again as she chanted something to herself.

She opened her eyes sharply and pulled away, dropping her hands from my temples. Immediately the swirling smoke dissipated. She faced Sinjin and arched her left eyebrow. "You're right. She has been the victim of an attack of magic through her unconscious mind," she announced simply.

"What does that mean?" I demanded.

She glanced in my direction. "It means that someone knew it would be easiest to plague you when you were sleeping."

"So?" I continued.

"So he or she infiltrated your mind with a dream, attacking you when you were at your weakest and leaving behind the sickness you're currently experiencing."

"So the dream was some sort of illness?" I asked.

Bella nodded. "Essentially, yes."

"Attack by witch or fae?" Sinjin asked, his voice laced with concern.

"I don't know," Bella responded.

"How advanced is her condition?"

She glanced at me again without even the slightest bit of concern in her expression. "It seems to be progressing rapidly."

"What can you do?" Sinjin insisted.

She shook her head. "I will need time."

"Time is a luxury we cannot afford," he barked.

Her jaw was tight. "In this case, you don't have a choice."

"What—" I started. "What is wrong with me?" My voice was rough as my heartbeat started escalating. I could feel my breath coming in short spurts.

"She should sleep," Bella said. "There is no use in keeping her awake."

"Charm her," Sinjin ordered as he turned to me again. He smiled sweetly as he held a hand to my forehead and ran his fingers down my temple to my cheek. Bella swallowed hard as she watched him, her eyes narrowing on me again.

She said nothing but faced me and never took her eyes from mine. Then she held up her hands, a white light glowing from them, as she said, "Sleep now."

My eyelids were instantly heavy. I fought to keep them open, though, since I wanted to understand more about what was happening to me. I'd never been so sick, seemingly deathbed sick. But it was no use. I began to succumb to Bella's power, my body falling into a deep sleep. My eyes were the last to give in to her power, and before I closed them, I caught the image of Bella looping her arms around Sinjin's neck as she smiled up at him, asking him when it would just be the two of them, when she would have him to herself again.

I never heard his response.

I was dreaming, some part of me well aware that I'd been charmed to sleep. Another part of me, however, somewhere in the back of my mind, remained awake. But it really made no difference because most of me was already lost in dreams.

These dreams were much more welcome than the last batch I'd been unfortunate enough to endure. Now I dreamed of a man with wavy brown hair and eyes of the same color. I could see him above me as he smiled, his dimples giving him a boyish sort of grin. There was rough stubble on his cheeks and chin that tickled when he kissed me. I giggled against him, and when he pulled back, proclaiming I was the most beautiful woman he'd ever seen, I just laughed and wrapped my arms around his neck, pulling him down to kiss me again.

We were outside in the sunshine, rolling and laughing in a field of heather. There was a certain crispness to the air, a salty mist brought over from the sea.

"Come with me, Jolie," the beautiful man said and stood up, reaching down for me. I put my small hands in his, and as he pulled me upright, I glanced down at myself to find I was wearing a white eyelet dress that came to my knees. The sleeves were long but did nothing to keep me from shivering in the brisk sea air.

"Where are we going?" I asked, brushing my long golden locks over my shoulder to find they were decorated with bluebells.

"It's not safe for you here," he answered as he pulled me close to hug me and I wondered what he could mean.

Then my handsome man began to fade right in front of me, right there in my arms. Soon he vanished into the air as if he'd never been there at all.

"Wait!" I screamed after him, alone in the cold air that was now surrounding me. "Come back!"

I felt my eyes pop open as confusion muddled my mind. I was no longer in the meadow with the beautiful man. Instead I was in my bedroom, and the garish sun was forcing itself through my windows, blinding me with its intensity. I tried to identify the shadow of a person sitting in a chair beside me, blinking a few times against the intrusive sun, waiting for my pupils to constrict. When they did, I half wished they hadn't.

"Bella?" I asked, sounding puzzled.

"You've been asleep for half the day," she responded in her usual irritated tone.

"What are you doing here?" I continued in a feeble voice, feeling as if my head was going to split in two. Exhaustion and weakness were consuming me, just as they had the night before. I couldn't even lift my head.

"Sinjin put me on duty while he rests," she responded and began inspecting her nails.

I nodded and closed my eyes again, feeling even sicker than the night before. As soon as my eyelashes touched my upper cheeks, I heard something. At first it sounded far off and muffled, but the more I focused on it, the clearer it became.

Jolie.

It was a man's voice and a voice I knew, a voice that I suddenly felt I had known forever. It was the voice of the man in the meadow, and I had to wonder if I were dreaming again. I opened my eyes to test the theory but found Bella sitting beside me, glaring at her phone as she texted someone. No, I definitely wasn't dreaming.

Yes, I thought the word, testing to see if it was in my head. *Who are you?*

Rand, the voice said and a flush of warmth crept through my body, overwhelming me with the sensations of safety and happiness.

He is your enemy, came my next thought but I shook it away as something within me, something bigger and stronger, insisted that Rand was not my enemy and never had been.

Listen to me, Jolie, his voice said. *You must trust me or you're going to die. I can heal you—I'm a warlock and I have that ability.*

But you're my enemy! You're dangerous.

You know that isn't the truth! Trust me.

How are you in my head? I asked, suddenly feeling even more exhausted.

It is the connection we share, one we've always shared. He paused for a second or two. *It's just a small link of our bond.*

I didn't understand what he meant so I didn't respond.

I can feel your weakness, Jolie. I can feel your illness.

I swallowed hard, not even bothering to wonder how that was possible, much less how we were having a telepathic conversation. I just chalked it up to my fevered mind, which was just as sick as my body. *I don't know what's wrong with me,* I answered in my mind's voice.

I am coming for you, he said. *We can heal you.*

I didn't have the strength to wonder who "we" meant and let it go. Instead, I felt relief flooding me at the thought of seeing him again, feeling his arms around me, knowing that I was safe.

Are you alone? he asked.

No, Bella is here.

There was silence for a moment or two, and I could feel the beginnings of anger welling up within me. A split second later I knew it wasn't my own anger I was experiencing but Rand's. It was, as he said, our connection.

You must send Bella away, Jolie. You must think up a diversion.

I swallowed hard but figuratively nodded.

When she is gone, contact me again, he finished.

How?

Just think the words, the same as you're doing now.

I breathed out a large breath and tried to imagine a way to get rid of Bella. What could possibly send her away? At first, I drew a blank; then it came to me.

I opened my eyes. "I feel something," I said, my voice hollow, pained.

"What?" she demanded with little or no interest, continuing to fiddle with her phone.

"Sinjin, I feel like there's something wrong with him," I finished and smiled inwardly once I realized I had her attention.

"What do you mean?"

I shook my head and sighed, feeling exhaustion beginning to claim me again. It took all the energy I had just to speak. "I don't know. I just . . . have a bad feeling about him. Can you . . . can you go check on him?"

She narrowed her eyes, but something in them hinted that my words worried her. "He told me not to leave your side."

"Please, Bella, I just feel something . . . bad about him, like something's . . . happened to him."

She stood up and threw her purse over her shoulder. "I'll be back," she said before disappearing into my hallway.

I smiled as I closed my eyes and reached out for Rand. *Rand! Can you hear me?* I thought the words.

Yes, I heard in my head. *Did you manage to get rid of her?*

She's leaving but you'll only have twenty minutes, at the most.

I am already on my way, he said, and then our connection was lost. I smiled to myself before clenching my eyes tightly as another headache hammered me.

It felt as if mere minutes had passed when I heard footsteps. I opened my eyes and found Rand before me. He was wearing dark jeans and a white T-shirt that contrasted against his tan skin, making him literally glow with healthiness. It was the same outfit, I suddenly realized, that he'd been wearing in my dream.

"Jolie," he whispered.

"I don't know what's wrong," I started but he brought his fingers to my lips and silenced me.

"You must sleep, Jolie. When you wake, everything will be fine again. I will see to it." His words must have acted like a spell because I suddenly felt myself falling back into the seas of sleep, cresting the waves of dreams.

FIVE

"I think she's coming to."

There were voices—three of them, one woman and two men. And they all sounded tense. I could hear the sound of pacing—footsteps going to the far end of the room and back again, only to repeat themselves. I groaned as I opened my eyes and rolled my head to the side, feeling the prick of goose down from the pillow my head was currently lying on. I rolled my head upright again and spotted a thatched ceiling just above me. I had to still be dreaming.

"Jolie?" It was Rand's voice.

I turned my head and my focus went blurry as I tried to look at him. He hurried to me from across the room and I guessed he was the "pacer" I had heard walking back and forth when I woke up. He appeared as a brown blur at first, but after a few seconds, this delineated itself into the insanely handsome man I was coming to know. "What . . . what happened?" I asked.

He grasped my hand as he smiled down at me. His smile reminded me of the dream I'd had when we were kissing in the heather, feeling the sea breeze wrap around us and caring about nothing besides each other.

"We've healed you," he said softly before turning to face someone else in the room. "Mathilda?"

I glanced beyond him at the little old woman who was now hobbling up to my side. There was something about her that was also familiar—something that tugged at my memory. She smiled down at me and held her hands above my face. I felt my eyes focusing on the lines etched in her skin, hinting at just how old she was. That was when it hit me. She was the same old woman who had come into my store. Just like the first time I'd met her, she was wearing the same ill-fitting, outdated long dress, and her hair was just as unruly in its extreme length. And she still possessed that same aura of age-old beauty.

"The block has been removed," she said simply as she dropped her hands, turning to take a seat just beside the bed.

"But . . . ," I started, still staring at her. "You . . . you were in my store."

"Yes, child," she said and smiled softly, her voice again reminding me of the ringing of bells. "Yes, that was I."

"You're a witch?" I asked as I focused on the blaze of blue light emanating from her. How had I missed it before? I tried to remember if there had been any indication she was otherworldly when I first met her. Try as I might, though, I could think of nothing.

She shook her head and Rand patted my hand, pulling my attention back to him. "No, Jolie. Mathilda is one of the oldest and wisest of the fae."

"The fae," I repeated, shaking my head as doubt seized me. "You mean, like a fairy?"

"Aye," a man's voice called from the corner of the room. I craned my head and swallowed hard at the vision of an incredibly tall, broad, muscular man who stepped out in front of me. "I am Odran," he said simply.

"Odran is the King of the fae," Rand said, smiling as I regarded the King of the fae with openmouthed astonishment. He was just so . . . so . . . big! Big and beautiful . . . stunningly so. His long blond hair fell about him in a mass of waves, pale against the bronze of his body. His eyes reflected the tan color of his skin, flecked with rays of amber. He was wearing nothing but a kilt, and his chest, though riddled with muscles, was completely hairless. His face and overall stature seemed reminiscent of a lion.

And that was when feelings of dread descended on me. I was completely at their mercy now. If Rand and Mathilda had evil intentions where I was concerned, I was as good as dead. God, I'd been so stupid. Why had I trusted them? Why had I allowed myself to get into this predicament?

Because you were dying and Rand saved you, my conscience announced.

So what, maybe he just saved me so he can kill me later.

You know that isn't true.

Well, you can't tell me what the truth is so why listen to you anyway? And dammit all, how is Sinjin going to find me?

I turned to face Rand again, needing to know where I was and what was happening. "I don't understand what's happened and where I am . . ."

"Ye are in oone ah me villages, lass," Odran responded in a thick Scottish brogue. It was as if he'd crawled off the cover of one of those Highlander romance novels they sold at the grocery store.

"Jolie, I will explain all of this to you in time but suffice it to say you're safe now. No one can harm you."

I closed my eyes and swallowed down the relief that suddenly washed over me at his words. Relief that was immediately replaced with fear.

No one knows where I am.

I felt like I wanted to sit up again. Rand tried to hold me down but I adamantly shook my head. Admitting I'd won the tacit argument, he assisted me. He pushed the pillow behind my back so I could prop myself against it. "Am I still in Los Angeles?" I asked, wondering where a fairy village could exist in the city.

Rand shook his head. "No, we're in the sequoia forest."

I swallowed hard. "The what?" I asked, thinking to myself that the sequoias had been a good four-hour drive the last time I'd ventured up there. And that had to mean that at least four hours had passed since I blacked out at my house . . . Oh my God. Four hours!

"All fae villages exist in forests," Rand continued, but I couldn't say my mind was on the habitation and villages of fae.

"How long have I been here?" I inquired, my voice laced with worry.

Rand nodded in understanding and when he spoke, his voice was soft, compassionate. "A day."

"A day?" I repeated, shaking my head. How could I have been out of it for a whole day? And furthermore, what was going through Sinjin's mind? He must be worried sick because as far as he was concerned, I'd basically vanished. I swallowed down the worry that suddenly plagued me and tried to think of a way back. "I've been asleep all this time?"

Mathilda nodded. "You had to overcome the magical block, child," she said.

"What is a magical block?" I demanded, feeling as if the weight of the world was now descending on my shoulders. I didn't know what any of this meant, nor what to make of it.

"Your sickness was of magical origins, Jolie," Rand explained, taking my hand and rubbing it as if that could help ease my frazzled nerves.

"Whose magic?"

"Well, we aren't exactly sure, just yet," he admitted. "All we know is that you had a magical block in place that made you very sick. We were able to remove it; but in order for you to regain your strength, you need your rest."

At the thought that they expected me to stay here and "rest," I started to freak out. I needed to get back to Sinjin, to let him know I was okay. "I can't stay here," I protested. "Sinjin . . ." But at the expression on Rand's face at the mention of my vampire, the words died right on my tongue.

Rand swallowed hard. "Jolie, you will come to realize that Sinjin is not the person you believe him to be."

I shook my head, not wanting to listen to Rand's words, refusing to believe there was any truth to them. He just didn't understand the connection between Sinjin and me—Sinjin was my protector, my teacher. "He has no idea I'm here."

Rand took a deep breath. "No, he does not."

Even though there was something within me that had let Rand in, and allowed him to come to my aid while I sat wasting away in front of Bella, I couldn't say that I trusted him. Not while my heart still belonged to Sinjin. Not while I still believed in Sinjin.

"I know this is a lot for you to take in," Rand started.

"I don't trust you. I don't believe that everything you say is true."

Rand was quiet for a second or two, and then I heard his voice in my head.

I don't know how I can prove anything to you, Jolie. But what I can tell you is that you and I have a long, shared history.

If that's true, I thought back, *tell me something about myself that you shouldn't know.*

He was quiet for a second or two and then smiled victoriously. *Your father is dead and you were never close to your mother. You once told me that she just didn't understand you—she never had, perhaps because she was too involved in religion to understand the fact that you could see things that didn't make sense. And you have been able to see auras since you were a small child.*

I took a deep breath but said nothing, stunned by his statement. Everything he'd just said was true. The only other person who knew any of it was Christa. True, he could have somehow bewitched Christa into spilling the beans, but I somehow doubted it. He just seemed so genuine.

"Please, Jolie, just trust me, this will all make sense to you shortly," he said. "For now, I need you to rest and regain your strength."

I was incredibly worried, especially as I thought about Sinjin waking to find me gone and not knowing where to even begin looking for me. Rand's words must have acted as some sort of magical command, though, because I felt myself suddenly relaxing, lying back on the bed. He helped me get comfortable, fluffing the pillow before I dropped my head on it. I took a deep breath, realizing I could breathe much more easily now. The headache had vanished. Even though I still felt tired, it wasn't the same sort of aching exhaustion I felt before with Bella. "What was wrong with me?" I asked, my voice already heavy with sleep.

"We do not know for certain, although we believe it was Lurker magic," Mathilda responded.

"Lurker," I repeated, starting to sit up as realization dawned on me. Rand immediately pushed me back down again.

"You need to rest, Jolie," he said softly.

"Lurkers . . . That was the word that kept going through my head during those dreams," I said as I battled with my heavy eyelids. "They are rallying, building their numbers. They're going to attack us."

"Dreams?" Rand repeated and glanced up at Mathilda, a question in his eyes. "That's how they must have attacked her."

"In exactly the same fashion they did the first time," Mathilda added.

"What first time?" I started just as I felt myself drop off only to wake up with a start a second later. "What are you talking about?"

"Jolie, tell me about this dream you had," Rand said. Then he added, "Awake unless I tell you otherwise."

The exhaustion that was relentlessly trying to claim me instantly vanished. I took a deep breath, thinking about the dream images, feeling fear begin to bubble up within me once again. "There was a battlefield with dead soldiers; and others who were still alive, in combat. None of them was human—they were witches, vampires, and the fae, I think. Then I saw a throne with a crown and a scepter. Both the scepter and the crown later melted into the throne." I glanced at Rand with an expression that said I was at a loss as to the rest of the images.

"I see," Rand said softly and smiled at me.

"What did you mean by the 'first time' I had this dream?" I asked, turning to face Mathilda.

She glanced at Rand as if seeking his approval to answer, but he shook his head. "We will explain everything in time, Jolie, but for now, I just want you to sleep."

Before I fell back into unconsciousness, I caught an expression of worry that passed over Rand's face as he eyed Mathilda and Odran.

"The dreams were one and the same" were Mathilda's last words before I lost the struggle and drifted to sweet sleep.

When I woke up, it was dark. I opened my eyes and saw the same thatched ceiling. Sitting up, I yawned with relief as I realized I felt completely healthy again. The intense sickness I'd experienced was now just a distant memory. Discovering I'd been left unattended, I stood up and stretched my arms over my head, wondering if the feelings of dizziness would return. But they didn't. Encouraged, I took a few steps, still testing my body. But I was fine. One hundred percent restored to my former self.

Glancing around, I took in my strange accommodations—there was a stone fireplace in one corner, with a little wooden stool placed before it, somehow welcoming in its austerity. Looking up from the fireplace, I noticed a circular window, complete with muslin drapes on either side. Outside the circular window were flowers of a species I'd never before seen. They were lemon yellow and as tall as me. I continued scanning the room, taking in the dirt floor, which was covered by a large rug that looked to have been woven of straw. The furniture in the room, including a bed and a table with two small chairs, was completely constructed of hand-hewn logs.

I heard the door open and turned to face my visitor, tension riding up my neck. When I realized it was Rand, the tension disappeared, replaced by relief. Well, that was until I remembered Sinjin had no idea where I was and that I was basically being held hostage. Yet something within me still didn't believe it—it felt as if I were right where I was meant to be. "You have a lot to explain," I said simply.

"Are you feeling better then?" he asked as he handed me a wooden mug of what appeared to be water. I accepted it but didn't bring it to my mouth, just swirled the contents around in the cup.

"I feel like I'm back to my old self," I announced and glanced up at him with a slight smile of thanks. I couldn't deny that I had a lot to thank this man for—namely for restoring my health.

Yeah, but you also have to think about the fact that you are now Rand's pawn, that he has you right where he wants you and Sinjin has no idea where you are, I reminded myself.

I dropped my gaze to the mug in my hands and studied the contents, wondering what he'd brought me.

"It's water," Rand said softly.

Suddenly feeling parched, I held the wooden mug to my lips and drank. It tasted strange—almost like well water, as if it hadn't been treated by any sort of plant, which I guess made sense since we were out in the boonies otherwise known as fae.

"I do want to explain everything to you, Jolie," Rand continued. "Are you feeling well enough to listen?"

I nodded and sat down on my bed, as if to prove that I was ready and willing to hear his side of things. I needed to understand what sort of threat the Lurkers were and what my dream signified. Rand took a seat beside me and smiled. It was strange, but I could suddenly feel the heat radiating from him, heat that was such a contrast with the coldness of Sinjin's skin. I had to swallow down the sudden urge to feel Rand's warmth on my skin, to taste him and experience for myself what it meant to be with someone supernatural who shared my own temperature.

"I can explain everything to you or I can do you one better," he started.

"What do you mean?" I asked as I eyed him suspiciously.

He chuckled at my expression and shook his head, never taking his eyes from mine. "With the help of fae magic, I can restore all your true memories to you, Jolie. Things can be as they were always meant to be." He paused. "Or as close as possible, given the circumstances."

"My true memories?" I started, already lost. "What true memories?"

He nodded and took a deep breath, as if realizing he needed to go back to the beginning. "Everything that you know is not how it really was," he started.

"You've said that before. I don't understand what you mean."

He nodded and was quiet as he apparently searched for the right words. "Jolie, Sinjin broke the rules—he altered history. He was never supposed to walk into your store that day. It was supposed to be me." Rand's gaze never left mine. "Jolie, I met you before Sinjin did."

I shook my head. He'd told me this before too. "But that isn't the truth!" I took a deep breath, trying to understand what he was telling me, and make sense of it somehow. "How? Explain to me how?" I insisted.

"Because Sinjin sent himself back in time to ensure that he would meet you first."

"How is that even possible?"

"I have learned to stop asking myself that question. We are creatures of magic, Jolie." He paused for a second or two and offered me an apologetic smile. "Anything is possible."

I took another deep breath. "So just playing devil's advocate here for a second, let's suppose that I believe you about Sinjin wanting to go back in time and meeting me before you ever got the chance to . . ." Was I really even considering this craziness? "What would be the reason? Why would he even bother in the first place? I mean, I can't imagine time traveling is as easy as getting on a bus or something?"

Rand shook his head. "You just don't get it, Jolie."

"Get what?" I asked and sighed. "What is there to get?"

He took each of my hands and stared at me. As much as I felt like maybe I should pull away, I couldn't. "Jolie, you are incredibly powerful. So powerful that all sorts of creatures want to control you or at least have you on their side."

I swallowed hard, anger and pain assaulting me at the same time. I tried to figure out where Rand was going with all this. "So you're saying Sinjin wanted to control me too?"

Rand frowned and dropped his gaze, as if he didn't want to witness the pain that I'm sure was building in my eyes. "I think so, yes."

If everything Rand had just said was true, it suddenly cast my relationship with Sinjin in a new light. It made me feel as if I might be sick. Why? Because it made total sense. I'd always wondered what Sinjin saw in me—the girl next door who definitely didn't stand out in a crowd. And he was so regal and handsome, so dashing and completely out of my league.

Or, on the other hand, this could be Rand's way of getting me on his side—weaving doubt about the truth of Sinjin's affections for me. Maybe I was playing right into Rand's hands by doubting the person who was my true protector, the person who had come into my life for the express purpose of keeping me safe.

I exhaled a pent-up breath of pain and frustration as I felt tears stinging my eyes. Which was it? Was Sinjin just using me or was Rand hoping to take his place?

"Sinjin was never good enough for you. He never deserved you," Rand said and placed his hand on mine, squeezing it reassuringly. Then he sighed. "I once promised myself that I would do everything in my power to ensure that Sinjin never hurt you, and I'm afraid I failed."

I swallowed hard, trying to fight the need to believe him, but somehow I couldn't. It was as if there was a crack in the foundation of my feelings for Sinjin and that crack was spreading, turning into a valley of doubt. I looked up at Rand, all the while aware that he was watching me. "How do we get my memories back?"

An hour or so later, I was standing in the middle of my cottage room surrounded by people—well, by the fae. Mathilda had instructed Rand that the spell would only work if there was enough magic.

I was nervous as I listened to the hushed voices of the twenty or so as they assembled in the room. It sounded like a hive of bees all nervously buzzing about. I felt an arm around my shoulders and glanced up to find Rand smiling down at me. I wasn't sure why but this time-traveling thing was beginning to grow on me. Maybe there was something to it. Maybe Rand had been telling the truth all along.

Well, whatever the outcome, all I knew was that I was fed up with all the second-guessing—of Sinjin, of Rand, even of myself. Maybe that was the reason I'd agreed to this so-called memory spell—I needed to know the truth, whatever it was.

"So what happens if this doesn't work?" I asked, feeling both agitated and frightened.

Rand shrugged. "Then I suppose it just doesn't work."

"This spell won't take my current memories away?"

He shook his head. "No, everything you know now will remain the same. All this is intended to do is return to you everything you knew before—

all your experiences, your feelings, your memories."

I watched Mathilda enter the room and all the voices around us became silent as she parted the sea of fairies and proceeded toward Rand and me. I wasn't sure why, but at the sight of her, my heart raced. She reached for my hand and I willingly offered it to her. Then she smiled at me so serenely, I felt any nervous energy fade away.

"This should not take long, child," she said in her soft cadence. "And when it is done, you will understand everything . . . It will all be clear."

I nodded at her and thought how wonderful that sounded—how I wanted now, more than ever before, to no longer feel as if I were always the last to know, as if I'd been completely left out in the dark.

Mathilda turned to face everyone in the room and smiled broadly. "I thank you all for coming and for doing so on such short notice. I understand that many of you have traveled from Britain, as did our generous and kind King." Then she glanced at Odran and bowed. I looked at Rand and mouthed, "How did they get here so fast?" I mean, last time I checked, a flight from the UK to California took at least ten hours.

He just smiled at me and said—in my head, I might add—*Fairy magic—they can travel much more quickly than humans can.*

Oh, I thought in return and faced Mathilda again. I could feel Rand's gaze as it lingered on me. When I turned back to him, he just smiled in that handsome way of his.

"Please join hands," Mathilda said. Those in the room formed a circle around the three of us, each of them taking the hand of the person on either side of them. "This is one of the most difficult charms to perform," she continued. "It will require your absolute focus and strength. Please close your eyes."

Mathilda reached for my hand and Rand's at the same time that Rand reached for my other hand. I felt his familiar electricity course up my arm but it didn't cause me any discomfort. No, now I felt as if I was on the brink of something wonderful, of coming home again, as crazy as that sounds.

"Focus on sending all your magic, your power, into Jolie," Mathilda instructed, closing her eyes and tightening her hold on my hand. "Rand, I need your concentration the most," she whispered.

"Of course," he responded.

"Focus on your feelings toward her, on everything you have shared together, everything you have experienced. Think of emotions as well as actual events."

He just nodded. Mathilda opened her eyes, facing me. "You must open yourself, child, open yourself and accept all the power that is offered to you. Embrace it and make it your own."

I didn't know what that meant but nodded anyway, figuring I could just do my best. Mathilda closed her eyes again and started chanting something indecipherable, her mouth twitching with the effort. I looked at Rand and found that he too had his eyes closed tightly.

That was when it hit me. And it hit me like a truck. I suddenly felt as if my entire body were being swept up in a typhoon, my feelings and emotions battling one another, only to sink into my subconscious. It was like puzzle pieces circling before me in a great wind, some falling down to find their place in the puzzle that was beginning to take shape—the puzzle that reflected my life—a life that I had no clue ever existed.

As strange as it sounds, I felt like I was filling up. It was as if there were a void within me that was now growing solid. And while there was no pain, there was tremendous pressure on my very being, on my soul. Little by little, I began to fill up from the inside out. Thoughts and emotions ran through me that I didn't understand as experiences I had no familiarity with began to build within me.

I clenched my eyes tightly as images came, one after another. I watched Rand walk into my store that fateful day, just as he'd said. Then that memory was whisked away, to be replaced with Rand teaching me how to take the shape of the beast— but I was only able to assume the shape of a fox. Another vision dropped in front of that one, this one of Rand dressed in nineteenth-century garb—from a time when I'd traveled back to 1878 and fallen in love with him all over again. Memories continued to pummel me, images of Rand on the battlefield of Culloden in Scotland when we'd gone up against Bella's forces, Rand in the drawing room of my home in Scotland, Kinloch Kirk, where we'd planned my future as Queen, and Rand inside me when we'd first bonded . . .

I opened my eyes, my breathing elevated as my heart pounded in my chest. At the point when I felt I could handle no more, Mathilda dropped my hand. I glanced at her then, seeing her in a new light. I felt as if I had known her for years. She looked at me curiously.

"Mathilda," I said with a smile, tears glistening in my eyes.

She responded with a wonderful grin. That was when I remembered his hand still clenched in mine. It felt like slow motion as I turned around and my eyes settled on the one man whom I had loved so completely for the past two years—the one man who had made me what I was today.

"Rand," I whispered.

SIX

I felt as if I'd just awakened from an incredibly long and frustrating nightmare and finally landed in the realm of clarity. It was almost as if I'd been living in a hallway of closed doors, wondering at what could possibly be behind each one, and now every door was open, inviting me to explore.

It was just like Rand said it would be—I'd retained my most recent memories but now I had a whole shelf of memories layered above them, some complete contradictions, which I assumed were due to Sinjin's manipulation of time. Even though there were still unanswered questions, and I had to force myself to remember the truth in several events, I felt complete again. And that feeling of wholeness created a sense of serenity and contentedness within me.

"Jolie," Rand said, and I returned my attention to his beautiful face, his caring eyes and loving expression. I was faintly aware that he and I were now completely alone. I wasn't sure when it happened, but everyone in the room was gone, allowing us to rekindle our love in privacy.

"Did Mathilda's charm work?" he asked, his tone hopeful.

I simply nodded, smiling up at him. Her charm had worked, and then some. But while looking at him, I completely lost control of myself and felt a sob strangling my throat as my eyes unleashed a deluge of tears. Instantly, Rand's arms were around me and I buried my face in his shoulder, inhaling his clean, masculine scent. I held on to him as hard as I could, never wanting to let him go—never again wanting to think of him as my enemy . . .

My enemy.

I pulled away and looked up, into his beautiful chocolate eyes. "I'm so sorry," I started. "I'm so sorry for not trusting you, for not believing everything you said.

I . . ." I shook my head, feeling so completely disgusted with myself for the way I'd treated this man. He was the one who cared for me so completely that he'd traveled through time in order to find me again. "I feel horrible about everything that's happened between us."

He shook his head, a smile claiming his sumptuous lips. "None of that matters now, Jolie," he said and held me closer. "You didn't know me from anyone and everything you did or said was completely understandable. And I'm sure Sinjin didn't help matters."

Ire began to grow inside me at how Sinjin had completely manipulated the situation: how he'd openly lied to me about Rand, declaring that he was dangerous and wanted only to control my powers, and ultimately me. I was suddenly able to see Sinjin for the absolute manipulative asshole he was.

Do you really believe that was all there was to it though, Jolie? my inner voice sounded. *Could there have been more to the role Sinjin played in all this?*

Of course I believe it! He changed the course of history to ensure his place next to the Queen.

But you've always known Sinjin had feelings for you. And there were moments when he seemed to genuinely care for you . . .

He's a good actor but that's it!

You know it's not as simple as that, Jolie. You know Sinjin better than that. He wasn't always thinking about the throne. You're lying to yourself if you think Sinjin was just out for himself.

How can I believe for one second that I meant anything to him? All he wanted was to control me, with the ultimate hope of getting closer to the crown.

You can't believe that. You know he's more complicated than that.

Okay, so he also wanted a good romp in the sheets.

A feeling of sickness suddenly passed over me as the memory of having sex with Sinjin hit me like a bomb. And then the shock was replaced with fury. It was bad enough that Sinjin had ripped me away from Rand, had reversed the natural order of things for his own selfish reasons; this was the ultimate icing on the cake. He'd not only taken advantage of the situation, but he'd taken advantage of me, my heart and my body. He'd always wanted to know me as intimately as Rand had. Somehow this was the ultimate blow, making the pain inside me suddenly worse.

You're feeling this way because the pain is still so raw, that voice continued, driving me crazy with its need to defend Sinjin.

I'm feeling this way because I should be feeling this way! And regardless of what you think, what it comes down to is what Sinjin did wrong—he had no right to tear me away from everything I knew and loved. I can't see past that.

My other voice was finally silenced. Not that it mattered anyway because I was fully convinced that all my thoughts should be focused on Rand and how happy I was to be fully restored to him.

I laid my head against his chest as I listened to his heartbeat. He was so broad and warm. I just wanted to lose myself in the beauty of the moment. But I knew I couldn't, because so many questions were cycling through my mind—there was just so much that had happened, so much I needed to better understand.

"Rand?"

"Yes?"

"How were you able to come back and find me?" I asked, remembering the last time I'd talked with him before this whole time-travel incident had happened. I'd been in my home, Kinloch Kirk, and Plum, my cat, had just squeezed through the door. I'd gone after her and, in the process, happened to glance down at the beach just beyond the cliffs of Kinloch. What I'd witnessed there not only shocked but profoundly disturbed me. Standing on the beach had been Sinjin and the prophetess, Mercedes Berg. But observing them wasn't the cause of the fear and angst within me. It was what Mercedes and Sinjin were in the midst of doing—an incantation. I recognized Mercedes' preparations for the spell immediately—mainly because I'd undergone the same one with her before, when she arranged for the two of us to leave 1878 and return to modern times. Once I'd realized what they were up to—

time traveling—I'd used my telekinetic abilities to reach Rand and tell him exactly what was happening. I'd begged him to find Mathilda as quickly as possible. And that was all I remembered . . .

He was quiet for a few seconds as he took a deep breath. "When I found Mathilda and explained what Mercedes and Sinjin were up to, she was able to harness some of Mercedes' residual charm."

I shook my head, already confused. "What do you mean?"

"When a charm is performed, the molecules of energy that aren't utilized in the charm float away into the air. The farther they get from other charmed molecules, the less potent they become, eventually dissolving into nothing. Mathilda was able to weave a magical net whereby all the residual energy from Mercedes' charm was harnessed by Mathilda. That allowed us to return to this time and place, just as Sinjin did."

I nodded, thinking his explanation made sense. I sighed as I recalled the visual of Mercedes on the beach with Sinjin, trying to understand why she would have ever agreed to send him back in time. Mercedes was not someone I would consider my enemy—quite the contrary. She was my advisor in all things related to my kingdom.

She was also my mentor, someone who helped me in my struggle to grasp my duties as Queen of the Underworld. I had relied on her, as well as valued and trusted her.

"Why would Mercedes do this to me?" I asked.

Rand cocked his head to the side and was quiet for a few seconds. "I don't know," he said in a harsh tone, betraying the fact that he held Mercedes responsible for everything that had happened. I couldn't imagine she was his favorite person at the moment. "I believe Mercedes, herself, is the only person who can answer that question."

One thing was certain—there was no way Mercedes had agreed to such a plan merely to grant Sinjin a favor. Sinjin meant nothing to her. I was fairly sure she didn't even like him. No, there had to be another reason why she'd done what she had . . .

"The prophetess should never be doubted." I heard Mathilda's voice from the corner of the room and felt my breath cut short. How long she'd been sitting there was anyone's guess—it was as if she'd just materialized from thin air because I was convinced Rand and I had been alone only minutes earlier. She stood up and approached us, wearing a placid smile.

"So you believe we should still trust her?" Rand asked with a frown. "On the face of it, it appears she has already teamed up with Sinjin."

Mathilda shook her head. "The actions of the prophetess are much more black and white, Rand," she said softly. "The monarchy is the only priority the prophetess has. She exists only for the betterment of the Underworld society, and even though we may not comprehend her motivations, we must, nonetheless, trust in her judgment."

"Blindly?" Rand asked, his tone betraying the fact that he disagreed.

Mathilda nodded, flashing Rand a frown as her eyes burned. "The prophetess seeks to protect the monarchy, to protect the Queen," Mathilda finished. Hmmm, just as Mercedes existed solely to protect the kingdom, so Mathilda would always protect Mercedes.

"She has a damn funny way of showing it," I muttered.

"And Sinjin," Rand started, anger returning to his tone. "What do you propose we do with him?"

Mathilda's gaze focused on something outside the window, as if she were picturing Sinjin in her mind's eye. "The vampire should be punished."

"Punished here and now? Or when we return to our own time?" Rand persisted.

"Return to the present?" I asked, never considering until that moment what our plan would be. "Those molecules you collected—are there more?"

Mathilda smiled up at me. "Yes, they are forever ensnared in my magical web."

Then something occurred to me. "Would it be better to remain here?" I asked, just tossing the possibility up for consideration. "If anything, it would allow us more time to build our legions against the Lurkers." Another thought occurred to me. "And we could nip Bella's rebellion in the bud, stopping it before it ever got started."

And furthermore, I thought, I would never have to die on the battlefield . . . which also meant I would never find Mercedes . . . "We have to return to the present time because the battle with Bella has to occur, or Mercedes can never be freed from the year 1878."

Although speculation regarding the existence of the prophetess had always been alive and well throughout the Underworld community, no one had ever laid eyes on Mercedes. Why? Simply because she was trapped in time, in 1878, reliving each day because otherwise she'd be killed off by Lurkers, according to a vision Mercedes had had.

In the war against Bella's forces, while I lay in Rand's arms dying, Mercedes had usurped control of my own magic, thus saving me at the same time that she brought me back to 1878. And once there, through the use of our mutual powers, we had been able to travel back to the present time, saving Mercedes from a fate at the hands of the Lurkers.

"We must return," Mathilda said flatly, staring at Rand. "And we must bring the vampire."

I swallowed hard at the mention of Sinjin, thoughts of hurt and disappointment returning once again, pricking me just as freshly as they had the first time.

"Sinjin should be staked," Rand said with finality.

"No." I heard the word leave my mouth without being aware I said it. But there was something within me that rebelled at the thought of killing Sinjin—making him pay the ultimate price for his offenses.

Rand faced me with a frown but was spared the obligation of responding when Mathilda cleared her throat, shaking her head. "We cannot condemn him as we know not what motivated him. And until we do, we must avoid making judgment."

I said nothing more, although inside my emotions were in an uproar. Of course, I didn't think Sinjin deserved to be killed—he hadn't done anything that unforgivable. And as far as anyone knew, he'd acted with Mercedes' support. No, I didn't believe he should be put to death for his transgressions. But I also couldn't help my feelings of devastation, not wanting to admit that even though he'd wronged me, I was still very much in love with him. That was the unfortunate part about retaining all my most recent memories. Of course, now that love was also being mitigated with anger and distrust. But there was no point in crying over something that was never anything in the first place. No, I would shelve all the pain and the anger and move on. Even though I still stupidly loved Sinjin, I also couldn't deny that I was deeply in love with Rand. And Rand was the right choice, the only choice.

I glanced over at Rand and smiled, reaching for his hand. He folded mine in his and smiled back down at me. I felt a shard of guilt. How could I ever have been able to love another man when Rand was my true heart's connection? I took a deep breath and shook thoughts of Sinjin right out of my head. There was no use in focusing on him ever again, nor wasting any more of my energy. I mean, I'd already wasted more than enough of myself on Sinjin. Now I would, instead, focus on the issues at hand.

I took another deep breath, turning back to the laundry list of items to discuss. This time I glanced up at Rand. "I was able to take the shape of more than one animal when I called on my sister beast," I started.

"You called your inner beast?" Rand reiterated as worry began to well up behind his eyes.

And so I explained it all to him, which led to a discussion about just what I was if I wasn't a witch. And of course that conversation really led nowhere because no one had a definitive answer for me. So I just figured it would go unanswered at least for the time being.

Another mystery I was able to put to bed was how Mathilda had been able to restore my full memories to me. When we'd attempted a similar charm in 1878, Mathilda had only been able to restore feelings rather than actual memories. The answer was that Mathilda hadn't been the fairy then that she was now, because "one never stopped learning, and one's magic never stopped advancing." And that made sense. Her magic must have grown by leaps and bounds in over a century.

"I think you should rest for a bit, Jolie," Rand suddenly announced. "You have been through a great deal and we have all the time in the world to answer your questions."

I shook my head, feeling as if there was just so much I needed to know, not to mention the catching up I needed to do. But Rand faced me and his lips were fi rm. It was the expression he wore whenever he didn't want me to argue with him.

"If you are going to attempt to help us travel back in time, you will need your strength," Mathilda added with a nod of her silver head.

"When are we even going to attempt this?" I asked, glancing first at Rand and then at Mathilda.

Mathilda was quiet for a few moments, presumably considering the question. "We have many preparations to make ahead of time. First, we must locate the vampire."

"Why?" Rand demanded. "He existed in the present time, before we traveled to the past, so he should continue to exist when we return."

"It is not quite so simple," Mathilda responded. "If he remains here, he could wreak all kinds of havoc if left unattended." She stood up. "I grow weary and will now take my leave of you both."

I didn't say anything else but just nodded and watched Mathilda open the door to my little ramshackle cottage and close it behind her. Then I faced Rand, unprepared when he suddenly pulled me into his arms and kissed me. His kiss was demanding, passionate, and I met his thrusting tongue as I wrapped my arms around his neck.

He pulled away from me then and stared down at me, his expression flustered as his breathing came in quick gasps. "I need to make love to you," he whispered.

I felt something catch inside me at his words and a fi re began building. He brought his lips back to mine, kissing me as if it would make up for the multiple weeks when he must have been going out of his mind with frustration and disappointment.

I felt his hands beneath my shirt, squeezing my breasts. A groan rose up from his throat as he did so. He pushed aside my bra and found my stiffened nipples, pulling his lips from mine as he knelt and took one of my breasts in his mouth. I moaned against him just as the image of Sinjin intruded on my mind.

A shudder flashed through me.

"Rand," I said, suddenly feeling sick to my stomach. I pulled his face up from my breast and started to blush at what I was about to say to him. But there was no going back. I simply couldn't make love to Rand when my feelings were so chaotic and up in the air. I couldn't make love to Rand when I was still in love with Sinjin.

"I can't do this," I whispered.

"Can't do this?" he repeated, his tone revealing how thrown he was by my change of demeanor. Thrown and disappointed.

"I just . . . It's just too soon," I said and adjusted my bra back in place while I smoothed my T-shirt down, refusing to glance up into Rand's face. I was afraid of the disappointment and pain that would probably be in his eyes. Rand wasn't an idiot. He had to know where this was coming from.

"Look at me, Jolie," he said in a small voice. I felt my breath stop as I glanced up and caught his eyes. He gazed at me for a few seconds, as if he were trying to make sense of what I'd said. Then something made him glower and shadowed his mood and I knew he'd figured it out.

"Because of Sinjin?"

I closed my eyes at his words, hating to admit it—hating the fact that Sinjin owned a part of my heart, my soul. But it was, nevertheless, the truth. Until I could straighten out my messy emotional allegiances, I needed time to myself. I needed to retreat and heal. It wasn't right for me to give myself to Rand, not while I wasn't a whole person.

"I'm sorry," I said softly, reaching out to touch him as if that would make it all better. But he backed away from me, and my hand merely dropped to my side.

"Are you—" he started as he ran an agitated hand through his hair. "Are you in love with him?"

I took a deep breath, afraid to answer the question. But, finally realizing I had to answer it, I did. "Rand,

I . . . I don't know what to tell you, what you want me to say. I love you just as much as I always have . . ." "But you love him too," he finished for me and shook his head. "Even after what he's done to you?"

I took a deep breath. "That certainly changes things, but love doesn't just turn itself off so easily, Rand. Even if he . . . he broke my heart."

Rand nodded and turned soft eyes on me as he did so. "I understand," he said simply and started for the door.

"Rand," I stopped him even though I wasn't sure what more I should say. It seemed as if the damage was already done. "Eventually this won't be a problem for us."

"I understand," he said again, and before he turned to leave, he faced me again, worry gnawing at his features. He bit his lip as if he didn't want the words to come out of his mouth, but eventually, he opened his mouth and asked me: "Did you sleep with him?"

I swallowed hard and that was enough for Rand. He sighed and opened the door, disappearing into the cold fae night.

SEVEN

I couldn't sleep.

For the last four hours since Rand had left me, I'd been tossing and turning, wondering whether or not I should have been so forthcoming with Rand regarding my feelings for Sinjin. I mean, the last thing I wanted to do was hurt him—and by the look in his eyes before he walked out of my room last night, he'd been hurt and then some. If those thoughts weren't enough to keep me wide awake, reflections of Sinjin continued to plague me.

I kept replaying memories of Sinjin over and over in my head, wondering how he could have been so cold and calculating when he appeared to have really cared about me. The things he said, the way he acted—I fell for his whole charade hook, line, and blood drinker.

"Ugh," I groaned as I forced myself out of bed. I was in my house again, but only after insisting that I needed to go home to sort out my thoughts. Rand, acting as his normal overly protective self, argued with me, of course, but in the end my donkey obstinacy won out.

Figuring sleep would continue to elude me and needing a diversion for myself, I decided I was thirsty. I threw on my robe and stepped into my slippers, plodding off to the kitchen. Today I would head over to Sinjin's house to see if he was still there. If he was, I'd let Rand know so he could arrange to have Sinjin's casket, or whatever it was that the vampire slept in, moved . . . as in, into the future with us. And if Sinjin wasn't around, as I'd imagined he wouldn't be, I was just going to continue living my life as usual and basically wait around until he found me.

When he eventually did come to me, I was going to play dumb and act as though I had no idea where I'd been for the past day or so. Like I had amnesia. Then, of course, he would have to enlist the help of the "benevolent Bella" to ascertain just what in the hell happened to me. Then the two of them, like the Bobbsey Twins, would try and figure out whodunit.

Well, that was the plan, but I didn't feel like sticking to it. No, I didn't feel like playing some idiotic game with Sinjin where I had to pretend I wasn't livid with him and that I had no idea there was a huge knife in my back, thanks to him. Instead, I had my own plan. And that plan revolved around demanding answers from him—as his Queen, I had the position as well as the authority to do so.

There was no reason for me to wait until tonight to put my new and improved plan into action. As it was, I couldn't sleep and had nothing else to do . . .

With iron resolve, I forgot about the glass of water and, instead, hightailed it back into my bedroom. I pulled open my dresser drawers as I searched for a pair of jeans and my pink UCLA sweatshirt. I threw both on in record time and, eyeing my disheveled hair in the mirror, opted for my white baseball cap.

"All right, you bastard," I whispered. "The time of reckoning is here."

I grabbed my purse and keys from the kitchen counter before starting for my garage. Yes, it did occur to me that it was probably a better idea to wait for Sinjin to come to me, but I didn't care. He probably wouldn't be there anyway. At the moment, I just had to escape for a little bit, to get out of the house. And I couldn't wait any longer to demand Sinjin tell me what he really wanted from me and why he'd altered the course of history to get it.

Opening the door to the Jetta, I buckled myself in and turned on the engine, waiting for the garage door to lift. Then I started getting nervous.

What if Sinjin is at his house? What are you going to say to him? I thought to myself. *Are you just going to blaze in there with your guns drawn? Or are you going to be more subtle about it?*

I don't know, but it doesn't really matter. Whatever happens, happens.

Chances are, he won't even be there anyway.

Well, he'd better be because it's going to drive me crazy to have to sit and wait for him to come to me! No, I need to get this done and out of my system, and pronto!

I'd been so involved with my mental conversation, I nearly missed my cell phone ringing from deep inside my purse. I reached over and played treasure hunt for a few seconds before I finally grasped my phone and pulled it out. I recognized Christa on the caller ID immediately. I also realized it was past midnight but figured she'd just gotten home from a date or the fact that I was missing was keeping her up late.

"Sorry, Chris," I said as I answered. I suddenly realized that I'd virtually disappeared off the face of the planet for the last couple of days and hadn't gotten in touch with her at all. Bad friend.

"Um, where the hell have you been?" she asked, her tone heated.

I sighed as I put the car in reverse and, while balancing the phone on my shoulder, attempted to back out. "It's a really long story, Chris, and I don't have time to tell you now."

"Where are you?"

I took a deep breath, putting the car in drive as I started down my street. "I'm on my way to Sinjin's."

"God, I thought he'd finally eaten you," she said as she exhaled a pent-up breath. "I figured you caught him on a bad day, when he was really hungry, and I was this close to calling the police. Good thing for you the only thing stopping me was that I would have sounded like a whacked-out, crazy bitch."

Even though she was completely serious, I couldn't help my laugh.

"This isn't a joke, Jolie!" she railed. "You need to reconsider dating him! He's a vampire, for crying out loud!"

"You're just now realizing this?" I muttered. She was still so caught up in her tirade, she didn't even hear me.

"I mean, it's not like the pig dates the farmer or the slop dates the pig."

"What?" I asked, shaking my head, as I turned on Sinjin's street. The familiarity of the pepper trees caused a sadness to root in my gut.

"Food hierarchy, Jolie," she said, the essence of *duh* in her tone. "You don't date your food."

"I'm not Sinjin's food," I pointed out. "Well, not yet, I hope."

I cleared my throat as I figured I ought to tell her the truth about Sinjin and me. "And anyway, Sinjin and I broke up."

"Then why are you on your way to his house?"

"Like I said before, it's a long story and one I can't tell you right now because I'm already here."

She sighed, long and deep, and fake for emphasis. "Okay, but promise me you aren't going to go all psycho on him and beg him to take you back or some crap. Remember to stay strong, Sista Sledge."

I shook my head at the very idea of begging him to take me back. No, things were beyond over between us. "I promise."

"Okay. Be safe, Jolie." She paused for a second or two. "I've invested a good twenty years into you, you know? Don't go and die on me now."

I laughed, thinking Christa had the strangest way of expressing herself. But if anyone stuck by me through the good and the bad, she did. "I'll be safe, Chris, don't worry."

Then we said our goodbyes and I hung up the phone, taking a deep breath as I faced Sinjin's house. None of the lights were on, but that wasn't what snatched my attention. It was the for sale sign out front with a picture of the real estate agent who'd sold him the house.

So I was right: Sinjin had already moved on.

All hope inside me sank. As soon as I spotted that sign, something in me suddenly became heavy; it almost felt like I was drowning. I'm not sure why I didn't just turn around and go home, but I didn't. Instead, I just sat there with the motor running as I stared at Sinjin's house and allowed the happy memories of our time together to suffuse me.

That was when I promised myself I would beat this; I would beat this depression, or at least the feeling that a part of me was suffocating, dying. Yes, I would beat this— I was already on my way. The love I felt for Sinjin would crumble into nothing and eventually be blown away, dissolving into the air like the unused molecules in one of Mercedes' spells.

"Goodbye," I whispered to the house. But somehow, I felt the driving need to turn off the car and walk up to the house, just to see if it was completely vacant, or still full of furniture. I wanted to ensure that Sinjin really had given up the house in the same way that he would soon abandon me once he learned I had all my memories back.

Stop trying to kid yourself. The only reason you want to go up there is to feel close to Sinjin again and it's a stupid thing to do.

I ignored that voice and turned off the engine. Now I was just sitting here, in the dark, arguing with myself.

You might as well just go up there. I mean, it's dumb just sitting here and staring at his house like a lovesick dumb-ass.

He's already gone, so what's the point? You're just going to freeze your ass off.

You're still sitting here . . . Crap and a half!

"Ugh," I said at last as I undid my seat belt, throwing open the door. The cold night air assaulted my legs through my jeans and I shivered.

I stood up, not wanting to dally any longer. I was just going to go look through the living room window and see if there was any furniture. The only reason was to report back to Rand and Mathilda.

Okay? I asked my inner voice.

Okay.

Good. Fine. Done.

I ran across the street and felt my heartbeat pounding in my throat as I started up Sinjin's walkway. I felt a general depression again as I glanced around myself, thinking how everything had appeared in such a different light the last time I ventured up this path. Before, things seemed fresh and promising; and now, this was the beginning of the end.

I pushed my melancholy thoughts aside and tiptoed over the grass as I leaned against the living room window, cupping my hands on either side of my face, hoping to ward off the glare from the streetlights.

His house was empty.

I'd been expecting it, but the sight depressed me all the same. Sinjin had really packed up and moved out. He was just as aware as I was that whatever existed between us was dead and gone.

"Funny meeting you here."

I almost didn't believe it was his voice; but somehow, I knew I hadn't imagined it. I felt like I was stuck in sand as I turned around to face him. I didn't say anything right away, mentally begging my heart to calm down, but it adamantly refused. Sinjin appeared more beautiful than I'd ever seen him. He seemed taller somehow, and broader. His hair was just as wavy as it normally was, with the ends curling up over his collar; and there was that wicked gleam in his beautiful blue eyes. He was every inch the devil's henchman.

"Sinjin." I said his name as if it were a curse and tried to shake myself out of my dreamlike stupor. I wasn't sure if I was seeing him in a different light because I now had multilayered memories of him, which allowed us a much deeper connection, or if I'd merely missed him. Either way, I couldn't help the breath that was stuck in my throat or my unabashed stare. Yep, I was standing there like a complete idiot.

And that was when I remembered: I remembered that Sinjin had been using me all along, that he'd thwarted my pursuit of a happy life with Rand by changing the course of history, that he'd worked tirelessly to ensure that I would fall fast and hard for him, and that the whole thing had been completely calculated, entirely choreographed, and utterly false.

I reminded myself that Sinjin Sinclair never cared for me. But most of all, I remembered that he'd broken my heart.

Something inside of me erupted, and fueled by his assholish smirk, I unleashed the palm of my hand against his cheek. His head turned to the side with the impact and, when he faced me again, his left eyebrow was elevated as if to ask, *What else do you have up your sleeve?* But his fangs were indenting his lower lip, indicating that he wasn't exactly happy. I mean, I had to imagine it wasn't every day that a master vampire got bitch-slapped.

"Why did you do it, Sinjin?" I demanded, my voice hollow.

"Do what, love?" he asked as he continued to eye me with that look of amusement. There was no trace of pleasure, however, in the depths of his eyes. There was no trace of anything, actually.

"Spare us both the lies," I spat back. "I know what you did but I want to know why you did it."

"I have nothing to confess," he said resolutely, before his eyes turned hard as he studied me. "Perhaps you would care to tell me where you have been the past day and a half?" His voice was angry as he inquired, as if I were the perpetrator, the one who'd broken our bond.

I shook my head. Two could play at this game. "Answer the damn question."

He glanced at me with surprise showing through his gaze, as if he hadn't expected such vitriol, as if my anger was unwarranted. Then his eyes narrowed. "You seem different."

"*Different* is a good word for it," I said crossly. "Or another good way to describe it is that every memory I've ever had has finally been restored to me." His eyes widened only a fraction; if I hadn't been paying attention, I might not even have noticed. "Including the one when Rand first walked into my store two years ago."

Sinjin nodded as if he weren't alarmed by the news in the least, but he seemed to be struggling to appear indifferent. By now, I knew him well enough to know that he was anything but indifferent. How could he be when the control he sought so intensely was now dripping through his fingers like water? "And your current memories?"

"I have those too."

He chuckled without humor. "I should say Randall has matured into quite the warlock, do you not agree?"

I shook my head—I wouldn't be derailed. "Stop beating around the bush, Sinjin. You owe me the truth."

"The truth about what?" he demanded, suddenly dropping the charade of civility. He took a step closer to me until we were separated by nothing more than two inches. I could feel the chill of his body seeping into my bones.

"I want to know why you manipulated time to meet me before Rand did," I said fervently.

He shrugged. "Is it not obvious?"

"Say it."

He shrugged again, acting like this wasn't a big deal, like I had no reason to question him. "I merely wanted to meet you before Randall had the opportunity."

"To what end?"

He didn't respond right away, but smiled at me lazily. "That would be giving away my hand, love."

That was when I lost any patience I might have had. "You are a son of a bitch, Sinjin," I seethed and started to pivot on my toes and walk to my car. It was useless even talking to him—he'd never admit to anything. I didn't know why I had bothered to come here in the first place; it was a huge mistake.

"What difference does any of this make now, poppet?" he asked. I stopped walking and turned around to face him. "Your memories have been returned to you and you have a lovely life to look forward to with the warlock."

I shook my head, pain burning through me at his words. He was just so . . . cold. Tears began to flood my eyes, but I forced them back.

I would not cry. I would *not* cry. *I would not cry!*

"Do you really think it's that simple?" I managed to squeak out. I closed my eyes, taking a deep breath. "Maybe you've been alive for too long and you've forgotten what it is to feel; or maybe you're an absolute cold, manipulative fuckwad . . ."

Sinjin's icy chuckle interrupted me. I glanced at him furiously, watching him shake his head as he laughed, crossing his arms over his chest. Just as quickly as he started laughing, he stopped and stared at me through hardened eyes. "You think I cannot feel?" he demanded.

I took a deep breath but wasn't about to back down now. "I don't think you understand what it is to be human."

"Human? What will it take for you to understand that I am not human?"

"It's beginning to dawn on me," I grumbled.

"My humanity died the day I died," he snapped and his eyes were glowing red, incensed and angry. "But that does not mean I cannot feel."

That was when I lost it. A hurricane was building inside me that had finally gotten the thumbs-up to wage as much destruction as possible. I could feel the tears I was trying so hard to restrain suddenly come busting forward. Trying to avoid making a total ass of myself, I turned away from him and started walking toward my car, seeking nothing more than escape. I had to get away from him.

I should have known better. I should have known Sinjin would never allow me to retreat when I most wanted to. No, he got some sort of sick pleasure out of making me uncomfortable. So I wasn't surprised when I suddenly walked headlong into his chest and felt his hands grab my upper arms.

"I feel," he whispered, gravely. I made the mistake of glancing up into his face, which was so angelically beautiful—even if it hid a monster. He remained a creature of the dark that preyed on the weak not only for his sustenance, but to dehumanize them.

"You feel nothing," I said, narrowing my eyes and glaring at him. Tears were rolling down my cheeks, but at this point I didn't care.

His eyes were white.

His hold on my arms tightened as he gazed down at me. There was a curious expression on his face that I'd never seen before, something that seemed pensive, haunted, maybe even pained. "Look into my eyes and tell me again I do not feel anything," he demanded.

I swallowed hard and glared at him. "You manipulated me. You wanted nothing more than to exploit me so you could control the monarchy." I swallowed down a lump of regret and closed my eyes, willing my tears to subside. I opened them and found his gaze still riveted on mine. "You never cared about me. And the worst part of the whole stupid thing is that I thought we were friends, Sinjin. I thought you cared enough about me as a friend to never even consider doing everything you did."

"No," he started and emphatically shook his head.

"Don't belittle me, Sinjin, it's too late," I said, trying to free myself from his grasp. He refused to release me.

"I am not belittling you," he started but I wouldn't listen to him.

My eyes burned as I glowered at him. "I know you now for exactly what you are and I . . . I hate you."

For the first time ever, I saw a look of shock on Sinjin's face. He dropped my arms and I stepped away from him. He said nothing more. And there really wasn't anything more I either needed or wanted to say, so I started for my car. The tears were pouring from my eyes, and I felt like I needed to throw up.

"Did you think I would allow you to leave on that note?" he asked and I felt the coldness of his body right behind me. He gripped my arms again and yanked me around until I was facing him. I felt the air catch in my throat because there was just something off about him. It took me a few seconds to recognize the expression in his eyes as desperation. That was when it struck me—Sinjin knew everything he had worked so hard for was about to fall through the proverbial cracks.

But I didn't care. I refused to care.

"Let go of me," I seethed.

"Jolie, you do not understand," he said, his tone unequivocal, as his grip on my arms tightened. "You do not understand my reasons for what I did."

I shook my head and tried to extricate myself from his grasp, but his hands were like manacles. "You aren't going to talk yourself out of this one, Sinjin," I spat at him. "I know you for what you are, what you've been all along. I was just too stupid to pay attention even when you warned me yourself." I laughed incredulously. "I won't make the same mistake twice."

"Allow me to explain," he began.

"I'm not about to listen to you try to make this into something it isn't and never was." I took a deep breath, and when it appeared he had no intention of releasing me, I decided to pull rank on him. "As your Queen, I demand you release me."

He gritted his teeth and said nothing.

"I order you to release me," I repeated, realizing this errand had been a total waste of time. Sinjin would never admit the truth. If I were lucky enough to even get an explanation out of him, it would be biased, spun to make him out to be the good guy. I'd completely wasted my time.

"Is this how it will be between us, then?" he demanded, his fangs suddenly growing longer.

I held my chin up high and nodded. "Yes, Sinjin, this is how it will be between us. I am your sovereign and you are my subject." I never relished saying anything more than I did those words.

Sinjin said nothing but nodded and released me. I rubbed the blood back into my arms and caught my breath as I stared at him. There was one more piece of business we needed to discuss. And I wasn't about to back down now. "As your Queen, I order you to return with me to the present time—the time before Mercedes sent you back here."

He swallowed hard. "And how will you execute that without the prophetess?"

I smiled. "I have my ways."

He remained silent for a few seconds, just staring at me with an expression that defied description. It was like he was holding back—whatever words were on the tip of his tongue were stifled by his mouth.

"And when will our journey begin?" He glanced at the sky. "Dawn is near."

I nodded and hoped Rand and Mathilda would be ready. "Tonight."

"Very well."

"I want your word, Sinjin," I said. "I want your word that you won't skip out on your responsibilities and you'll show up tonight at my house as soon as the sun goes down."

He eyed me forlornly but then simply nodded. "You have my word."

I wasn't sure why, because I shouldn't have trusted Sinjin even remotely, considering the facts, but I believed him.

Figuring my mission was accomplished, I exhaled a pent-up breath and turned on my toes, heading for the Jetta.

"Everything that happened, every decision I made was to protect you," he said to my back.

I stopped walking and turned around to face him. "I would think you'd respect me enough not to feed me such a line of bullshit."

Sinjin's face was unreadable. "That is the truth. I never wanted to control or manipulate you. I merely acted as my role as sentry dictated. I was, am, and forever will be your protector."

And that was when all the anger and sadness hit me with the force of a truck. "You never wanted to manipulate me?" I said, my voice dripping with sarcasm. "Then why the hell did you make me fall in love with you and why the . . . fuck did you sleep with me?" I shook my head, hating the reminder.

Sinjin's expression didn't change. "Both events were logical outcomes of our closeness."

I shook my head. "Logical outcomes? Listen to how cold that sounds." I took a deep breath. "Sinjin, I wish you would just admit the truth for once and stop acting like I'm stupid."

"I am telling you the truth," he answered, his voice sounding suddenly tight.

"Please, Sinjin," I said, my voice cracking. "I'm not an idiot, contrary to what you obviously believe." Then I started for the car again.

"Whatever you think of my motivations is not true," he called out after me. "Everything I did was for you . . ."

But I didn't stop; I didn't even falter.

EIGHT

When I returned home, it was still dark. I probably had two hours of night left, and then the sun would crawl into her rightful place in the sky and I'd have one day left of what I now considered the present time. Was I worried about returning to the future? Yes, of course. As much as I trusted in Rand's and Mathilda's powers, abilities, and knowledge, there would always exist that undercurrent of doubt. That was just human nature.

When I pulled into my garage and turned the car off, I found myself zoning out again—as if I couldn't motivate myself to unbuckle my seat belt, open the door, and make my way into my house. I just felt exhausted, but at the same time adrenaline was pumping through me. Why? Because of Sinjin. I just had a sea of emotions roaring through me—anger and betrayal and, as much as it pained me to admit it, love. But all in all, seeing him had been good for me because it had, in a way, granted me closure. Even though he hadn't satisfactorily explained the reasons he'd manipulated both time and me, it didn't even matter, at this point. Maybe there was just a part of me that needed him to know I was completely aware of everything that had happened and there was no way I'd let him get away with it. And now that he knew, I felt like I could lick my wounds and heal. I could return to the future and be the Queen I needed to be.

And what was even more important, I could be the woman Rand needed me to be.

Sinjin, without even realizing it, had allowed me to get on with my life.

Jolie.

It was Rand's voice in my head.

I am so glad to hear your voice, I thought in response, feeling an overwhelming sense of warmth suffusing me. Rand was the one man whom I could openly trust, the one man who would never harm me. And it was his face that I pictured now and his face that I suddenly yearned to see.

I know you wanted some alone-time but I could feel that your mind was awake so I just wanted to make sure you were all right.

I felt myself beam. Rand had the ability to send mental mind feelers, as he called them, to see when I was awake and asleep. But that wasn't what made me all gushy inside. It was just nice to know that there was someone out there who genuinely cared about me, who wanted to ensure I was safe. Someone who sincerely loved me . . .

Thank you, Rand.

Thank you? And I wasn't sure how he did it but somehow his laugh transferred over our mind connection. His chuckle was deep and hearty and I loved the sound of it.

Thank you for always protecting me and believing in me and . . . for loving me just as I am.

He was silent for a few seconds. *Jolie, you don't have to thank me for any of that. It just is.*

Well, I'm thanking you anyway.

Is everything okay? he asked and then paused. *I'm worried about you.*

I quietly considered the question. *Things are as good as they can be, given the situation.* And as I finally unlocked the seat belt and opened my car door, I realized I was walking into my dark and lonely house, a thought that depressed me more than it should have. *Rand?*

Yes?

I paused, wondering exactly where he was. *Are you still in the fae village?*

No, I'm in a Hyatt up the street.

Up the street? I asked in surprise as something incredibly happy burst inside me. He was so close . . .

You know my worrisome nature; I didn't want to be so far from you in case something happened and you . . . needed me.

You should have just stayed with me, silly, I started.

No, you needed your space and I was happy to oblige you.

Oh, I thought and then took a deep breath, asking, *Well, I've had enough of my space for the time being. Do you want to . . . come over?*

I'd be happy to, he answered automatically, as if he'd been waiting for me to ask all along.

I smiled and, shutting the car door behind me, started for my house, feeling suddenly elated again. *Thank you,* I whispered in my mind. I absolutely meant it.

When I heard the knock on the front door twenty minutes later, I wasted no time in opening it. I just needed to see Rand, to throw my arms around him and tell him how much he meant to me, how much he'd always meant to me. I needed to wipe away the fact that I'd wounded him deeply and let him know how much I loved him.

I threw open the door and felt my breath catch when I beheld him. He was just so beautiful, so good. I stood there for a few minutes, staring at him, not able to say anything. He was wearing an off-white pullover sweater and dark blue jeans. His hair looked as if he'd just gotten it cut and he was freshly shaven, revealing the incredible lines of his jaw and the dimple in his chin.

"I never get used to how amazingly beautiful you are," I whispered.

"Me?" he said, smiling in surprise. "You're the one who makes my heart speed up every time I see you." He held his arms out and I rushed into them, wanting nothing more than to feel his warmth, inhale his spicy scent, and relish the sense of safety I always felt in his embrace. I rested my head against his chest, feeling like I was home, that Rand's arms were the only place I ever belonged or wanted to be.

"You don't know how much I've missed you," he said as he kissed the top of my head.

I pulled away from him and took his hand as I led him into my house, closing the door behind us. "I'm so sorry for everything that's happened, Rand," I said, shaking my head, loathing the guilt that was nearly choking me. "I never meant to hurt you, and I hate myself for doing it."

He glanced at me and took a seat on my sofa. "Jolie, you were honest with me. That's all I've ever asked of you."

I sat down beside him and took his hand in mine. "I know, but it kills me when I think about how you must be feeling."

He smiled sweetly, shaking his head. "It is what it is. It's not your fault that Sinjin used you to further his own ends."

I felt my stomach sink at his words, but they were the truth—Sinjin *had* used me to further his own ends, and that was exactly what I needed to focus on to heal the pain that still pulled me apart. Putting my anger aside for the moment, I focused on Rand again and noticed he was quiet, wholly focused on his hands, watching them knot into fists.

"I've dealt with my issues with Sinjin," I said softly, suddenly realizing how angry Rand was over the whole situation. As much as it pained me to hear that Sinjin exploited me for his own benefit, I was suddenly aware that it hurt Rand just as much to say it.

He glanced up at me, a question in his eyes. "What do you mean?"

I took a deep breath, knowing he wasn't going to like this part. "I saw him earlier."

He sat up straight, his eyes piercing as he stared down at me. "We were going to wait until daylight, I thought?"

I shook my head and stood up, walking to the kitchen to get a glass of water. I got one for Rand as well. After I filled each glass with ice and water, I braced myself and confronted Rand. His eyes were imploring, as if it was taking all his patience to sit quietly while I worked up my nerve to tell him what happened. "I couldn't wait, Rand," I admitted and then added, "I also didn't follow our plan."

Rand smirked as if he found the information as amusing as it was frustrating and raised a brow. "Why am I not surprised?"

I smiled at him in response and carried the glasses of water back over to my coffee table, putting mine down on a coaster while I handed Rand his. "I just couldn't pretend that I didn't know what he'd done," I rationalized. "I just couldn't give him the luxury of believing I was still ignorant, Rand. I wanted him to know that I was fully aware of what a total and complete asshole he is."

He nodded as if he couldn't find fault with the situation. "So what happened?"

I shrugged, memories of a few hours ago returning in a deluge of images. "I asked him why he did it but, of course, he refused to tell me."

"So he now knows you have your memories?"

I nodded. "Yes."

Rand stood up and ran his hands through his hair, showing that he was agitated, and started pacing back and forth. It was the same thing he always did when he was upset or frustrated. "Then he's going to try to leave town, now that he knows what our agenda is."

I shook my head even as I realized he wouldn't believe what I was about to say. "He gave me his word he wouldn't."

Rand turned to face me and there was surprise and irritation etched on his face. "His word, Jolie? His word is meaningless!"

I nodded, but I was steadfast in believing Sinjin wouldn't pull a fast one on me, on us. "I believe him, Rand. I told him to come to my house tonight at dusk and we would make our attempt to go home."

He glanced at me and exhaled, shaking his head at my apparent naïveté. "Then there is nothing left to do but wait and see if he keeps his word. I absolutely intend to be here, if and when he shows up," he said and took a deep breath. He was obviously being incredibly sweet for my sake;

I could tell he thought I'd just made a huge mistake. "Or perhaps we should go after him in the daylight and just take him with us, as originally planned."

I shook my head, well aware that the time for that plan was long gone because Sinjin was also. "No, he isn't living in his house anymore, and I don't know where his daytime resting place is."

Rand nodded and took a seat on my couch again, drumming his fingers along the top of his knee. "Then we will stick with your plan," he said and offered me an encouraging, hopeful smile. But I could tell he imagined it would take a miracle for Sinjin to actually keep his word and show up. Well, we'd have to see . . . "So it wasn't a wasted trip then?"

I shook my head as I considered it. "No, it wasn't. I got what I needed." I glanced at the glass in my hand, watching as the ice cracked in the water, beginning to melt. I looked up at Rand again and noticed that his eyes were narrowed on me. "I got closure."

His jaw was tight as he studied me. "I could kill him for hurting you."

I took a sip of my water, swallowing down any residual pain with thoughts of Sinjin. "What's done is done. It's in the past and we have an incredible future to look forward to together," I said with a smile.

I now wanted to focus only on what could be instead of what wasn't. Rand was absolutely the man for me. I knew we could be happy together.

He nodded and returned the smile but I could tell his mind was elsewhere, probably still on Sinjin if I had to guess. Then something must have occurred to him and he glanced up at me resolutely. "We could spare you all this pain, Jolie."

"What?" I asked, eyeing him with surprise. "What do you mean?"

He nodded again, as if the idea were becoming more appealing to him. "Mathilda and I could erase your memories of what Sinjin did. You would never remember you were ever . . . in love with him." He said the last four words like they caused a sour taste in his mouth.

I thought about it for a good few seconds because it did sound attractive—erase the anger and the pain and be able to think about Sinjin the way I always used to—as nothing more than a flirt. But then I knew I could never agree to it. I shook my head. "I can't. I need to know, I need to remember what Sinjin did, so I never trust him again. I need to recognize him for what he is."

Rand smiled at me as if to say he understood. "I just hate seeing you in pain."

I patted his hand. "I'm going to be okay, Rand. I just need time, that's all. And what's more, now that I know what Sinjin is capable of, I know the risk he poses."

"Keep your friends close and your enemies closer," he said and nodded.

That was when it hit me. Was Sinjin my enemy? I guessed in some ways he was. I mean, he had completely acted out of his own self-interest and could not have cared less where mine was concerned. As his Queen, would I have to punish him when we returned to the future? Of course, I had to impose some sort of punishment; it wasn't like I could just let him go. And, really, it wasn't like I even wanted to let him go. At times like these, I was glad I had the help of Mercedes.

Do you really have the help of Mercedes? I asked myself. *If she was in on this the whole time, then isn't she your enemy too?*

No, you have to listen to Mathilda on this one. Mercedes isn't to blame. You need to find out her motivation and trust in her. Remember that she will always protect the kingdom first.

"Was it painful to see him?" Rand asked.

I glanced at him, thankful to be pulled away from my inner dialogue as I considered his question. "It was painful," I answered and thought about how ridiculous this whole thing was because Rand had warned me about Sinjin so many times. He warned me never to get close to him, never to trust him, and I foolishly disregarded his advice. I once thought Sinjin was just misunderstood, that maybe I could break through his tough exterior to find some sort of goodness within him. I glanced up at Rand and smiled regretfully. "I should have listened to you all along. You were always right."

"It was your lesson to learn, Jolie," Rand answered. "And it just goes to show how good you are—that you give everyone the benefit of the doubt."

"Well, look where that got me."

He smiled at me and grabbed my shoulder, pulling me into the cocoon of his embrace. "It's one of the reasons I love you," he whispered.

"Has this whole thing . . . changed your feelings toward me at all?" I asked, suddenly afraid for his answer.

He pulled me into him more closely and held me, allowing me to listen to the beating of his heart as he ran his fingers through my hair. "Jolie, nothing could ever happen between us that would make me love you less."

And that was when I realized how incredibly lucky I was, how lucky I was to have this unbelievable man in my life. I didn't say anything but leaned up and cupped his cheek as I brought my lips to his. I didn't close my eyes—I wanted to see him, to soak in his male perfection. And he didn't close his eyes either; we both stared at each other as our tongues mingled. It soon became clear to me that kissing wasn't going to be enough . . . Sinjin had been the last man to make love to me, and that needed to be rectified.

I sat upright as I pulled the sweatshirt over my head and threw it on the sofa beside me. Rand glanced over at me in surprise, but I didn't miss a beat as I started removing my shirt. When I began to unhook my bra, Rand stopped me with a hand on my wrist.

"I don't want you to feel like you have to do this," he started.

But I interrupted him with a shake of my head. "I need to feel your claim again, Rand. I need for you to make love to me."

That was apparently all it took. He bolted forward and grabbed me in his arms, standing up as he carried me into the bedroom. I wrapped my arms around him and felt a shudder of excitement pulse through me at the thought of what was about to happen.

Once in my room, he gently laid me down on the bed and reached around my back, unclasping my bra. He slid it down each of my arms and seemed to take forever as he freed me from it and then he merely stared at my breasts as if he'd never seen them before, as if he were completely enchanted, mesmerized.

"You are the most beautiful woman I've ever seen," he whispered as he glanced up at me. "You have no idea how much you turn me on, how much you always have."

I just smiled at him in response and started to remove my jeans, unbuttoning them and pulling them down my legs. I wasn't interested in taking things slowly. No, now was the time for action. There was a fire burning within me that demanded fuel. I smiled up at him and grasped the bottom of his sweater, standing on my tiptoes as I wrenched it up and over his head. I was almost disappointed when I met his black undershirt rather than his gloriously naked chest and made a low grumbling noise in my throat to express my frustration.

Rand smiled down at me and, shaking his head in apparent amusement, removed the shirt himself, lifting it over his head as he gifted me with the view of his incredible biceps and even more incredible chest.

"When God was handing out muscles, you must have been in line twice," I said, awed.

Rand just chuckled and started unbuttoning his jeans. I watched him as he pulled them down his long legs and something became very clear. "But apparently you missed the line for boxer shorts."

He chuckled more heartily and I suddenly wished I had a camera so I could have recorded his stunning smile. He was just so incredibly gorgeous and genuine. What was more, he was mine.

"I was so eager to see you, apparently I forgot a few things," he admitted under his breath and seemed slightly embarrassed by the admission.

"A few things?" I repeated, cocking my eyebrow in question as I smiled.

He took off one shoe and held up his foot, revealing that he'd forgotten his socks as well as his boxers. I giggled and then took a deep breath as I glanced down the line of his incredible body, feeling him watch me as I did so. My gaze fixated on his erection and I dropped to my knees, grasping him in one hand while I took him in my mouth.

"Jolie," he moaned.

I watched him the entire time, watched him throw his head back as his eyes drifted closed, watched him undulate his hips against me. And he was pure masculine beauty to behold—utterly and impossibly powerful and strong and yet under my control, subject to my manipulation. He opened his eyes suddenly and pulled away from me.

"Your turn," he said quickly, but I shook my head. There was an urgency now rampaging through me that wouldn't allow any more time to go by without him inside me.

"No," I said. Freeing myself from my panties, I simply climbed onto the bed on my hands and knees and turned my head around to face him. "I need you now."

"My God," he whispered as he stared at my backside and swallowed hard. Then in another second, I felt the head of him at my entrance, threatening me with intense pleasure. I moaned against him and pushed back, encouraging him to seek shelter inside me, encouraging him to thrust.

And when he did, I was prepared for it even though it still took me by surprise. I moaned out and closed my eyes, feeling him pushing even deeper as he then withdrew and thrust again. And that was when I felt it, an unleashing of feelings deep within me. It was like every door to all my emotions was suddenly blown open; all the stores of sorrow and mourning from the time when I hadn't recognized Rand were now intermingling with the heightened feelings of love and absolute dedication that I felt toward him.

Like an explosion, it rained down within me, something emanating from the middle of my body and spreading at warp speed through the entirety of me. I clenched my eyes shut tightly and felt heat suddenly bubbling up within me—like the feeling you get when you drink something really hot on a cold day.

I opened my eyes and glanced down at myself, almost afraid that I was on fire, that something was happening to me. A thin, almost imperceptible white glow seemed to reverberate from my hands, climbing up my arms. When I glanced back at Rand, it was encompassing him too. I realized he had stopped moving within me, apparently having felt the same thing I was experiencing. The white glow encompassing us both began to grow, blinding as it emanated through the room. In another split second it was gone.

I pulled away from him and turned around until I was sitting on my knees, facing Rand, and was about to speak when I heard Rand's voice as clear as day in my head.

She's mine. She will always be mine.

That was when something occurred to me . . .

"Rand," I started, knowing what this meant and hoping we were ready for it, that he was okay with it. At that point, I also knew it didn't matter whether we thought we were ready for it, because it had already happened. It just *was*. This was nature's way of telling us that we were each other's soul mates—not even time would keep us apart.

It was suddenly incredibly clear that Rand and I were meant to be together.

"We're bonding," I said.

"I know," he whispered as he ran his finger down the side of my cheek. "I love you, Jolie. I've always loved you."

That was his way of saying he was okay with the fact that we were bonding. He was imprinting within me his indelible mark. We were joining in the ultimate fashion and would never, ever again be separated unless by death.

"I love you, too," I said and smiled as he reached for me and kissed me, pushing me back down against the bed as he settled himself between my thighs. At the feel of him thrusting within me, the subtle white glow began to return, bathing us both in its radiance. Rand thrust even harder as his emotions continued to feed into me and mine into him.

NINE

Rand and I were once again bonded, and all I could feel was happiness. I knew now, more than ever before, that Rand and I were meant to be together—we always had been. As for Sinjin? It was strange, but whenever I thought about the vampire or our brief time together, it was as if the feelings of pain and betrayal were replaced with numbness—as if I couldn't feel anything at all. I wasn't sure if the magic of Rand and my bonding had done something to eliminate any residual pain or angst that I felt toward Sinjin or if the numbness was due to my being completely head over heels in love with Rand. But I guess it didn't really matter anyway—what did matter was that I was no longer stinging from Sinjin's betrayal. Because of that, I could look at things clearly— without the taint of anger and pain that I'd felt before. I could see the situation and Sinjin for exactly what he was without the bias of unrequited love. It was important because as Queen, I needed to remain impartial and make decisions based purely on facts rather than emotion. I could now clearly recognize Sinjin for the manipulative and underhanded person he was without any of my emotional attachments getting in the way. And for that I was thankful.

Rand and I held each other for the remainder of the night and into the dawn, discussing our future together and how happy we were to have found each other again. The sun broke over the horizon and announced the next day was upon us. And that whole day moved like molasses. Rand returned to the fae village to escort Mathilda back to my house so she could help us with the time-traveling spell that evening. I decided to spend the day at my store so I could catch up with Christa. It was strange, but I felt I needed to say goodbye to her even though I knew we'd meet again in the future. It was probably silly, but something inside me wanted to see her before I attempted to time travel, to seek some sort of closure before I left.

For the entire day, I felt as if an enormous rock had taken up permanent residence in my gut. It made total sense, considering that the events this evening would change everything I knew, everything I'd ever known. Even though I had time-traveled before, those memories somehow seemed foreign to me, probably because I hadn't actually experienced them, even if the me of the future had. They just felt as if they weren't my own memories even though, of course, they were.

I didn't tell Christa anything about Rand, about our bonding, or that I was planning on traveling a couple of years into the future tonight. I just figured it would be too hard to explain and, furthermore, it would cause her undue worry. What did it matter anyway? Once I was back in the future, Christa wouldn't even know anything had happened. And what she didn't know definitely couldn't hurt her.

So we spent the day just making small talk, laughing about her myriad bad dates. When she finally asked me what happened between Sinjin and me, I just said I didn't want to talk about it; once I felt like I was over it, I'd explain. Luckily, she bought my excuse and left me alone.

That evening, I let Christa leave early for a date and closed up the shop just like I'd done a thousand times before. But, of course, tonight was different. Tonight would mark the last night I'd be in my store, in Los Angeles, in the United States! I must admit, however, there was something inside me that yearned for the tranquility of my home, Kinloch Kirk, nestled among the Scottish moors, perched high above the Eyemouth cliffs and pastures of wild heather. I couldn't help but feel as if I were saying goodbye to the life I had now. It was a feeling of sadness that deflated me, albeit tempered by excitement for the next chapter of my life, but sadness all the same.

As I swept the floors of the shop that had been a second home, I felt heavyhearted. I glanced around myself, taking in the worn sofas where my clients awaited their appointments, the Swiss cuckoo clock above the door that Christa had given me, the lettering across the window proclaiming my psychic abilities . . . It wasn't much, but it was mine. And my little business had allowed me to earn a decent living. It had paid for my home and a decently nice car. I'd really made something of myself here and it was hard to say goodbye. Even though I knew I was destined for much bigger and better things, it was hard to leave that part of me behind. I felt like I was saying goodbye to the old Jolie—the person who had no idea just who and what she was and the incredible things she'd soon experience.

The more I thought about it, the more I realized I was about to leave a much simpler time, a much simpler life. A life that was not only slower-paced but also safer, because I was more than aware of what awaited me in the future . . .

The Lurkers.

The realization frightened me. I'd be putting myself back into a dangerous situation. I was firmly aware that the Lurkers were an unknown; that was what made them such an absolute menace. Did they possess magic? Based on my visions of the throne and the battlefield, which attacked my magic twice, both in the future as well as the present, it seemed they did. That was a scary thought because we only ever thought of them as some form of pseudo-vampire and, as such, non-magical.

Vampire . . . Of course, my thoughts then turned to Sinjin and I stopped sweeping as I pictured him in my mind. Yes, there was still something sad in me over what had happened between us. I'd always been fond of Sinjin and now, more than ever before, I wished we could go back to how things used to be—when we were friends and cared about each other in our own awkward way. When I knew Sinjin to be nothing more than a harmless flirt.

He's anything but a harmless flirt, I reminded myself.

I know, but that doesn't mean I can't wish things were different.

I imagined the sadness I harbored over the deterioration of my friendship with Sinjin would always be there. It was a mere hiccup, though, compared with the agony I'd experienced when I first became aware of his manipulation.

I was healed. I wasn't sure how or why, but I was healed all the same.

I leaned the broom against the wall and took one last glance around me. Then I turned the lights off and opened the front door, stepping out into the burgeoning darkness. I faced the door and locked it, wondering what would become of my little store after I moved on. Maybe someone would open a donut shop or some sort of new-age boutique.

"Goodbye," I said as I took a deep breath and turned around, eyeing the stars twinkling in the night sky. The moon was full and already starting its journey over the earth.

"Poppet."

I turned at the sound of his voice and watched Sinjin walk up the sidewalk toward me. He appeared out of nowhere, almost as if the darkness had suddenly delivered him. The moonlight created a soft haze around him that made him seem like some sort of heavenly creature. But his dark attire, black hair, and piercing blue eyes said otherwise. The smirk on his full lips warned he was trouble and then some. At that point, more than ever before, I really regretted what had happened between us. I wanted to like Sinjin. But I had to repress those feelings because I couldn't like Sinjin; not anymore.

"I thought I told you to meet me at my house," I grumbled as I offered him a raised brow to say I wasn't amused.

His smile widened as he stopped directly before me. Then he merely glanced down at me and I was suddenly struck by how incredibly tall he was, and how much stronger than me. It wasn't a feeling that caused me any sort of fear, though, mainly because I was firmly convinced Sinjin would never hurt me. Why? I had no clue. Probably because I was an idiot.

"I beg the privilege of your company . . . alone," he said in a soft, deep voice.

"Why?" I asked as I started for my car, not wanting to encourage him in the least. "There's nothing left to say."

"Ah, that is where you are quite mistaken," he said, keeping pace with me.

We reached my car and I unlocked the doors with my remote. I opened the driver's door and took a seat, watching Sinjin as he continued to stand on the curb just beside me. "Well, are you coming?"

He smiled and materialized on the other side, opening the door and climbing into the passenger seat as he beamed over at me. "I did not realize it was an invitation."

I turned on the engine and glared at him, not wanting him to think he was in any way forgiven. "I wanted to make sure you weren't going to skip out on your responsibilities."

"I do recall giving you my word," he said and seemed rather put out, as if I should never have second-guessed him. Yeah, well, I was the new Jolie—the one who wouldn't trust as easily as the old one had.

I frowned. "Well, you're here so I guess that means you're good at keeping something." I glanced behind my shoulder to ensure no one was coming. When I found the coast clear, I pulled into the street.

"I never intended to hurt you," Sinjin said, and I could feel the weight of his gaze as it rested on me. I was never happier to be driving—to have an excuse for keeping my full attention on the traffic and pedestrians around me rather than the flagrant beauty of his eyes.

"I'm well aware of that, Sinjin," I said without offering him a sideways glance. "You wanted nothing more than to manipulate me, and making me fall in love with you was just part of your plan. So, no, hurting me was never your intention."

"You are wrong," he said tersely, never removing his eyes from me. "I have only ever wanted to protect you, to ensure your safety."

I stopped at a red light and glanced over at him, letting him know with one look that I was in no way amused and, furthermore, that I thought he was full of it and then some.

"I had taken a vow to protect you, in case you did not remember?" He was referring to a time in the future when Mercedes had appointed him as my bodyguard.

"Of course I remember," I snapped back at him. "And don't think for one second you're going to resume that role," I added.

He didn't say anything but cleared his throat in a way that said he wasn't happy with the news. "Regardless, I will forever be your protector."

"Sinjin, let's cut through the shit. Just admit that you were a complete and total asshole. Rand was right when he said you were selfish and had to manipulate every situation so that you always came out on top."

He gritted his teeth at the mention of Rand but then, just as quickly, assumed a more stoic expression. "I never denied that I seek situations of benefit to myself."

"Okay, now we're getting somewhere," I said, relieved. The light turned green so I faced forward and stepped on the gas. "So why continue with this line of bullshit about protecting me?"

"I merely stated the truth."

"Protecting me against what?" I demanded again, shaking my head with irritation.

"The Lurkers."

"What?" I glanced over at him. I couldn't help it.

"A car," he said simply and motioned ahead of us. I turned to face forward and had to brake hard in order to avoid the car stopped at the light ahead of me.

"Sorry," I muttered.

"Defending you from the Lurkers was why I went to the prophetess and requested that she send me back in time," he finished.

The shock of this news really jarred me. Sinjin, as a rule, never explained his reasons for his actions, so this was a huge surprise to say the least. "Why would you have asked that?" I turned left onto the freeway on-ramp and gazed over at him casually.

He was staring at me. "Have you not listened to a single word I have told you?" he demanded. I didn't respond so he continued. "I took a vow."

"So let me get this straight," I started, my tone relaying the fact that I wasn't buying his story. "You told Mercedes that you needed to go back in time to save me from the Lurkers? How does that even make sense? Why wouldn't you just send me back in time, instead of yourself?"

"It makes perfect sense," he said stiffly. "I intended to re-create history—knowing the future with the Lurkers and the threat they would pose, I told the prophetess that I would gain your trust and quash Bella's rebellion, thereby saving you from death."

"Which would also preclude me from saving Mercedes," I pointed out, none too nicely.

"That was merely a complication," Sinjin responded indifferently. "It was the reason I had Isabella tutor you, if you recall. Your power is enough that you could have saved the prophetess yourself, without her calling you into the past."

"Okay, so you wanted to save me from Bella and then what?"

"We intended to train you much faster to become Queen, to teach you what it meant to be the leader of the Underworld."

"And Rand?" I asked, my voice hollow.

"It would have spared you all the back-and-forth with him. The prophetess recognized the pain you suffered at the warlock's hands and was convinced it would have been better for you as well as the kingdom if he never ventured into your store that fateful day."

I remembered one of the last conversations I had with Mercedes before she sent Sinjin back in time. When I had begged her to send me back to 1878, so I could live out my life with Rand in a time when he loved me freely and I him. I felt my heart drop as I remembered how I'd told her how unhappy I was, how my relationship with Rand was coming undone . . .

It made perfect sense. Mercedes would always protect the kingdom, and that meant she would always protect me. Everything Sinjin said was true—Mercedes sent him back because she thought it would strengthen my allegiance to the crown instead of to Rand. She'd thought she was doing me a favor.

I felt like I wanted to be sick. I'd come so close to losing Rand—to never knowing him. I'd come so close to living a life I was never meant to live. But somehow, I couldn't be angry with Mercedes. I just accepted the fact, like Mathilda did, that Mercedes existed for the betterment of the crown. And she was the first to admit it.

Sinjin, on the other hand . . .

I exited the freeway and came to a stop sign before I was due to turn right. Once I braked, I glanced over at him. "I understand Mercedes' motivations in all of this, but you can't expect me to believe for one second that you were merely acting to protect me."

He swallowed hard and eyed me speculatively, a smirk playing with his lips. "Of course not."

Well, apparently this was diarrhea-of-the-mouth day for Sinjin because he was confessing things to me that I never, in a million years, would have imagined he would. "So?"

"I wanted to be first to meet you, poppet, for my own selfish reasons."

"Why?"

His eyes narrowed as he studied me. There was no traffic ahead of me, but I didn't make my turn. Instead I just stared at him, waiting for the moment of truth.

"I wanted you to love me."

I felt my heart rate increase, and something that felt like panic began stirring in my stomach. "Why?"

He was completely silent as he stared at me. It was as if he wanted to tell me but couldn't, like his voice went on strike or something.

"Why, Sinjin?" I prodded.

In a blink he was gone. He was there one second and a second later he dissolved into nothing, leaving me sitting in my car alone.

When I reached my house, there was a black Suburban I didn't recognize parked in my driveway. I pulled up behind it and turned off the car just as Rand stepped out of the driver's side and offered me a large smile.

I could feel his emotions as soon as we made eye contact. He was relieved to see me—in true Rand form, he was worried over the fact that I wasn't home and it was already dark.

We're going to have to work on your worrisome nature, I thought with a smile. He didn't respond but cocked a brow and regarded me with a grin.

"Hi," I said once he was in front of me. He didn't answer, just engulfed me in his arms, leaning down to place a chaste kiss on my mouth.

"Where have you been?" he asked as he squeezed me.

"I, uh, I was . . ."

But I never got the chance to finish my statement because Mathilda was suddenly beside me. Which was just as well because I wasn't sure how Rand would react to the fact that I'd been delayed by Sinjin. Speaking of the vampire, he was nowhere to be found.

"Child, are you ready?" Mathilda asked as she eyed me.

I took a deep breath, separating myself from Rand's embrace, and thought about the task at hand. "Yes, I'm ready."

"Where's Sinjin?" Rand demanded, looking around himself in an irritated sort of way. I could only guess whether or not Sinjin would show up after our conversation in the car. It seemed like he was on the threshold of confessing something that weighed pretty heavily on him—hence the whole disappearing act. Now whatever that something was would forever live in oblivion.

"I don't know," I said sheepishly, worried that Sinjin wasn't going to come through.

He'll come through, I told myself. *He gave you his word.*

"We need him," Mathilda responded, glaring at me impatiently.

"I knew this would happen," Rand said, shaking his head as he ran his hands through his hair. "We'll have to do this without him."

Mathilda shook her head adamantly, her silver tresses echoing her movements like ripples in a calm lake. "We cannot. Those who breached the laws of time to travel here must also return."

I felt something heavy settle within me as I thought about what a feat finding Sinjin would be. But it was pointless even contemplating it. If Sinjin didn't want to be found, he wouldn't be.

He gave you his word!

That was when I spotted him. He appeared at the end of the street, walking all nonchalant, as if he didn't have time—er, that is, history—waiting on him.

"Here he comes," I said, relief suffusing me.

He suddenly disappeared from sight, materializing just beside me. I breathed in my shock and felt my skin tingle with the cold chill that filled the air around him.

"Did you doubt me, my pet?" he asked and smiled, acting as if he were just now seeing me for the first time today, acting as if he hadn't nearly admitted to something very important, only moments before.

"Sort of," I answered, thinking it was closest to the truth.

"Poppet, you seem irritated with me." I hadn't noticed until just then that he hadn't spared a glance to anyone else in our party.

I took a deep breath. "I was wondering if you were going to come."

"I would not miss this for the world," he said, offering me a cheery grin.

"Let me make something perfectly clear to you, Sinjin," Rand interrupted, stepping forward when it seemed Sinjin was not going to acknowledge him. As I glanced at Rand, I could see the anger coloring his features—it was there in the reddish tone that bled across his cheeks, his neck, and the tops of his ears. His aura was electric blue, tinged with purple—something that only hinted at the incredible anger cresting through him. That was when I felt an eruption deep within me like lava overflowing into my stomach. It was Rand's rage.

"Ah, greetings to you as well, Randall," Sinjin said, not missing a beat.

"I believe you should face death for what you did to Jolie, your Queen," he said and took a deep breath, his eyes burning. "You have Jolie and Mathilda to thank for your life."

Sinjin said nothing to Rand, merely regarding him with ennui. Then he faced Mathilda and me and smiled. "Much obliged, kind ladies."

"He is here, we can continue with the preparations," Mathilda said, completely dismissing Sinjin as she turned to face me. "Do you have a garden, child? We will need nature's magic."

I nodded and led the way to my side gate, which would take us around my little house and into the backyard that boasted grass, roses, a lemon tree, and gardenias. Hopefully, that would be enough "nature" to fill Mathilda's needs.

"I hope you realize that punishment awaits you," Rand said to Sinjin as he reached over and took my hand.

"We shall see, Randall, we shall see," the vampire answered lackadaisically.

Mathilda eyed her surroundings, seeming to inspect my garden for its usefulness in her spell. She took a few steps to her right, then a few steps forward, until she was dead center in the grass with the foliage surrounding her. She looked up into the sky and seemed to be studying the moon.

"The orb is full, ripe for magic," she said, turning to face me. "Child, you must stand here."

She waited for me to approach her and took my hand, placing my feet exactly where hers had been. She motioned to Rand, took his hand, and positioned him to my right. Sinjin occupied the exact opposite position, to my left. Then she stood directly in front of me. She turned to Rand and extended her hand. He took it and she then faced Sinjin, doing the same. Then she addressed both of them.

"You must take each other's hands," she said unemotionally.

Rand grumbled something unintelligible but extended his hand. Sinjin grinned like this was all a big joke. Then I realized no one had taken my hand. "What about me?"

Mathilda faced me with a grim expression. "You are not returning," she said simply.

"What?" I demanded.

"Not returning?" Rand said at the same time.

Mathilda shook her head. "The Queen already exists in the future, having never time-traveled to the past. Only Rand, myself, and the vampire made the trip."

I couldn't argue. I hadn't time-traveled so, technically, I still existed in the future. Who knew what the heck would happen if I tried to travel with them now? Maybe I'd end up being two Jolies in one place or, worse yet, maybe time itself would freak out and spit me back into the dinosaur era, or the Spanish Inquisition.

"I understand," I said resolutely, afraid for what would happen once they traveled into the future. I wondered would the future just pick up where it left off when Sinjin and Mercedes cast that spell? It was too confusing to even consider.

"Are you sure?" Rand asked, staring first at Mathilda and then at me with wide eyes. "I don't want anything to happen to her."

Mathilda nodded but said nothing more. Then she took a deep breath and faced me. "I will unravel the net of magic; but your powers, child, more than any of ours, will enable this spell to take shape."

I nodded, feeling pleased I had all my memories. In having them restored, my experiences and my knowledge had been reinstated along with my powers. "What do I do?"

"Imagine a portal opening wide, the same portal you experienced when Mercedes sent you back into the present. Focus on that portal and keep it open. Allow each of us to travel beyond its frame."

I nodded. Over the course of my instruction and education in everything witchy, concentration and I had become damn good friends.

I love you, Jolie. It was Rand's voice in my head.

I caught his eye and smiled, taking a deep breath, trying to keep the tears at bay. He didn't need my tears right now—he needed my strength. *I will see you soon,* I thought in response.

I gave Rand one last smile and then closed my eyes and imagined a portal opening above us, a large black void that dominated the sky. I clenched my eyes shut tightly and saw the gossamer strands of Mathilda's web encapsulating the portal. What looked like raindrops caught in the ethereal threads, which were actually the captured essence from Mercedes' spell.

I felt energy bubbling up from within me, building momentum. In my mind's eye, I could see light escaping from my body, bathing me in a magical haze, increasing as every second ticked by, mounting as I continued to focus. The light shone from within me until I couldn't contain it any longer and, like an immense spotlight, it suddenly poured out of me, encompassing Rand, Sinjin, and Mathilda.

Then there was nothing but darkness.

TO BE CONTINUED IN:
WITCHING HOUR
AVAILABLE NOW!

ALSO BY HP MALLORY:

PARANOMAL WOMEN'S FICTION:
Haven Hollow
Misty Hollow
Gwen's Ghosts
Midlife Spirits

PARANORMAL & FANTASY ROMANCE:
Witch, Warlock & Vampire
Ever Dark Academy
Lily Harper
Dulcie O'Neil
Gates of the Underworld

PARANORMAL REVERSE HAREM:
My Five Kings
Happily Never After

CONTEMPORARY ROMANCE:
Age Gap Romance

SCI-FI ROMANCE:
The Alaskan Detective

Get FREE E-Books!
It's as easy as:

1. Go to my website: www.hpmallory.com
2. Sign up in the pop-up box or on the link at the top of the home page
3. Check your email!